HONOR GIRL

A Novel

By Alexandra Speck

© copyright November 2017

Preface

The love of my life broke up with me over a bowl of Honey Bunches of Oats.

"I know that someday, I'm going to need to be totally alone," Stephen said, slurping his vanilla soy milk. "I mean, all by myself..."

I said nothing, pretending not to hear and instead focused on the cereal box ingredients.

"Before I could ever get married," he continued, hammering the nail into our not-so-rosy coffin.

The only thing I could hear now was the deafening ring in my ears.

"Wait, what? Really? You don't think you can get married, unless you're alone first?"

I repeated his statement to clarify that what I heard was correct.

"Yeah. I just don't know myself at all... I am still just a boy."

A *boy*? As in like a cub scout? Was I seriously hearing this correctly? I mean, I knew he was 28, and four years younger than I, but I would hardly call 28 a boy...*Man-Baby* is more like it.

"Well," I said, feigning confidence, "Then you might as well be alone now. Why should we stay together, if I am just waiting for the axe to eventually fall, and we can't get married?" I called his bluff. This would show him.

"I'm sorry," he said looking down. He was trying to emote, just as he did while doing his monologue for theatre auditions.

"You're sorry? Wait...so this is, like, it?"

He didn't respond, just continued to look down.

I was aghast and floored. Was he planning for this to happen? What about all those nights we laughed talking about our wedding reception on Lake George, and how we'd float away on a kayak? What about the theatre company we had started and the plans to take our show on the road? It was all over. I hated everything about this shitty little Man-Baby, who used me for two years and ate up a very significant part of my 30s...I hated him.

Stephen got some of his stuff together--after finishing his cereal--and gave me a neutured friend hug at the door.

"Well, I guess I'll be touch," he said and shrugged his shoulders. "You can mail me the rest of my stuff."

"Mail you? Am I never seeing you again? Like, this is the final goodbye?" I asked.

"Well, I am not sure it's so good to see each other. It will make things harder. I need time to think," he said.

"Okay. Well, I guess…see ya," I said. I still didn't believe this was the last time I'd see him.

But it was.

He never called.

He never called again.

I waited and waited, thinking he'd take it all back, or get drunk one night and call me to tell me he missed me. Just three words: "I miss you."

But he never did.

He never called again.

My heart was broken.

I would never be the same.

Chapter 1

People say you only find love when you stop looking, and I think that's a big load of crap. I always looked, a constant search. Going to a coffee shop or a bar? I say do a quick perusal of the room, check out "the talent." If there's none to be found, grab your drink and keep it moving. Riding the subway? Imagine the man across from you sitting in a Burberry bathrobe doing the *New York Times* Sunday crossword puzzle, sharing his buttered croissant. If you're into him, or merely the idea of him, make some eye contact, refurbish your lip gloss.

If not, keep searching. That's at least what I think…because isn't it when you stop looking that you ultimately admit defeat--a life filled with cats, colorful tchatchkis, and grannie panties?

I lived in New York City for the bulk of my single life, and I was always in search of my one and only. Cynical as I may sound, I held true to the belief that you have one true love, a soul mate per se, and I always will. Despite the numerous flailed attempts at online dating, the overly soggy or under-ly scintillating kisses from frogs and princes alike, I was optimistic: he was out there. And, finally, one day, it seemed I found him. His name was Stephen…And I was happy, blissful even…Until it suddenly came to a crashing halt over a bowl of Honey Bunches of Oats. One year later, I was a poster child for Zoloft, donning sweat gear and elastic-waistband jog suits, one step closer to looking like my gym coach, and thousands of miles farther from New York City. I moved to Cape Cod, to a place called Woods Hole. And it wasn't what I'd expected. But, I was in for a surprise.

∧

I switched off the television and threw the remote control across the room.

Why?! Why must every time I turn on the TV, it's someone I know--or have known--or, even worse yet, dated. This time it was the latter-- it was my ex-boyfriend (whom I still was not over), Stephen. And he looked good too, adding salt to the wound.

"So, did you see it?" my friend Jeff asked, tearing into a popover from Pie in the Sky the next morning. "He must be doing really well if he's on *Scandal.*"

"Yeah... Um, what makes you think it's okay to say that?" I asked, unbuttoning my pants surreptitiously. (The muffin tops were not just for sale)

"You are not seriously bothered by this, are you?"

I did not respond.

"Emma, you broke up like 100 years ago. Besides, he looks swollen, like a tick." Jeff's lips glistened with bacon grease. "I was just saying relative--"

"Whatever... No, it's fine. I suppose I should be happy for him."

But I was not happy for Stephen. The truth is, up to that point in time, Stephen was the bane of my existence. He had ruined me, and not in a good way. I had essentially turned into a shell of a human being, to the point where

I had to "pull a geographic," or move, as they say in Alcoholics' Anonymous. (I only know this, because part of my hitting rock-bottom included about five daily glasses of Toasted Head Chardonnay, leading to my anonymous attendance at various AA meetings in church basements around New York City). In my quest to surface from being the bottom-feeder that I had become, I chose to move from New York City to Cape Cod. It seemed like a good idea--so natural, so "organic." I wanted to live the good life, a simpler life--walking the dog, collecting seashells on the beach, reading, having crunchy, down-to-earth friends, drinking red wine, finding my "authentic self," as Dr. Phil, my free therapist, would say.

But when I moved to Woods Hole, Massachusetts, it wasn't as I'd imagined. Well, I have to be honest--I'm not sure exactly what I imagined. I had been a summer resident, a.k.a. "tourist," growing up in Woods Hole. My father had a lab at The Marine Biological Laboratory there, doing cancer research on sand dollars and spider crabs. I always had fond memories of my teenage summers: ice block sledding on the hills of the The Golf Club, Coors Lite keggers and Nobska Beach bonfires, making out on the dock of the Woods Hole

Yacht Club. Granted, I was no longer a teen…but, maybe this place could be cool as an adult? After seven years as a struggling actress in New York, I was desperate for "normalcy"-- a barbecue, a deck, and even a small patch of grass in my backyard. I wanted a stable 9 to 5 job, direct deposit, benefits, shopping plazas. I wanted to get coffee in a drive-thru. I wanted anything but tall buildings, crowds, long lines and metro cards.

Now I know it's crazy that as a 30-something I was moving to Tumbleweeds USA. But, to my credit, I had done some research and read an article in *Boston* magazine that said Woods Hole was "the place to meet smart, intellectual men in their 20s." Granted, I wasn't in my 20s, but I could pass, right? Peter Pan complex, anyone? Unfortunately, once I got there, I exchanged my Peter Pan green tights for a pair of permanent, elastic waistband sweats, and I was living amidst a science experiment--literally--surrounded by clog-clad, crystal-wearing, NPR listeners. The hot men, I figured, must be lurking in the labs.

Now a small town has its benefits, like friendly faces (um, sometimes, not always) and maybe a free round of drinks at the local bar. But it also has its drawbacks, and isolation is one of them.

"I have *got* to get out of here. I'm rotting," I said to Jeff on the phone as I watched the snow fall heavily out my bedroom window and a coyote tip over my trash barrel. Jeff was my closest friend in town. I met him at the town market, called the The Food Buoy, buying a Stouffer's pepperoni French bread pizza the week I moved here. I've talked to him every day since.

"You're drunk," he said. "It'll be better tomorrow." Truthfully, I was a bit inebriated. So at least one part of my dreaming of Cape Cod life came true--drinking lots of red wine. I was a regular at the local packy.

"I'm totally not," I slurred. My tongue was thick and pasty. "I just hate everyone here. What happened to me?" I whined and fell back into my purple Calvin Klein comforter.

"Call me tomorrow," Jeff said, and he hung up the phone.

I turned off the light, grabbed my stuffed penguin and thought about what life would be like if I moved back to Manhattan.

Chapter 2

My move from New York seemed drastic to my friends and to my agent. I had been pursuing an acting career, semi-successfully, for six years. But I had hit a wall professionally. And personally, I was a mess. To me, the move made sense and was a must. But to my agent, well, that was a different story.

"You're what?" she screamed into the phone.

"Yeah, I'm leaving. Moving to the country. I just need a change," I said, staring at my unsigned lease that had been posted with a Winnie the Pooh magnet to my refrigerator for 60 days.

"Well, I mean, good for you, I guess. Call me when you get a refill on your meds and decide to come back," she said.

The reaction from my friends was not so civil either.

"This doesn't make any sense! You can't leave me here! I mean, a bad breakup is hardly worth dropping everything for," Kara said.

"It isn't just the breakup," I lied. "And there's nothing really happening that I can actually say I'm dropping."

"Well, you're dropping our friendship," she said. "Fine, whatever, Emma. When things get tough, you split. I know how this goes. Call me when you have a meltdown in the woods. I hope you don't end up like Jodie Foster in *Nell*."

Despite the lack of support from friends and family, I knew I couldn't stay any longer in Manhattan. There was no way I'd survive walking these same memory-filled streets. I felt I had done New York, and it had done me…in. And, yes, it was a very, very, very bad break-up--one that I felt I would never get over, not as long as I was living in New York. When Stephen dumped me after two and a half years, I wanted to die. And knowing he was alive and well, only streets away, and possibly dating some heinous troll, or even breathing, killed me. I imagined I'd run into him at every deli, or that I'd see him eating a fried sampler platter (our favorite) as I passed Empire Diner on 23rd and 10th late at night. And I began to avoid the places we frequented--Frank restaurant on 4th and 2nd, the Union Square dog run, Tavern on Jane, Murray's bagels. I cried myself to sleep each night, pining away for the days that I thought were the best in my life. I actually looked forward to my dreams because I could spend time with Stephen, time I no longer had. He was everything to me. I felt I had nothing left.

I met Stephen in the summer of 2004. I decided to take an acting class to work on my craft and to do something besides waitress and audition for roles in Off Off Broadway productions. I had gotten a commercial agent at this point and joined the Screen Actors Guild after doing a Bounty commercial, but I was still on the train to nowhere, and I needed a place to "work."

Stephen was that dark horse that I was drawn to— tormented, deep, and sensitive. I loved that he drank coffee and lived in a shitty apartment with a loft bed in his messy room and played guitar. I loved that he had a sick dog, a Dalmatian with cataracts and diabetes, for whom he'd cook chicken and feed it by hand and administer glucose shots twice daily. I loved everything about him, in a sick way.

When I first met Stephen in acting class, I had the opposite reaction. I hated him. He seemed arrogant, outspoken and affected. It was clear to me that he loved himself way too much and loved the sound of his own obstinate voice.

"I just think that my character wouldn't do that," he said, arguing with our instructor. "I'm going to do it my way. You'll see--it works better," he'd say.

So when I was assigned to work with him on an acting scene, where we'd have to get together and work outside of class, I felt dread.

On the night of our first rehearsal, I walked up the five flights of stairs in Stephens Hell's Kitchen apartment. The walls in the hallways were dingy-yellow, and there was an odor of something rotten. He greeted me at the door with his sick Dalmatian.

"Hey. Come on in." He smiled.

I could smell that he had just showered and applied Speed Stick deodorant. I was a sucker for men's deodorant smells. His soft black hair was still wet, and he had put some Suave product in it, which I found later in his bathroom. I think you can tell a man by his products. A Suave man, for example, is new to products and isn't willing to dole out more than a few bucks for something like "hair putty." He may not even know what the word "putty" means or its correct usage. Whereas, a Bumble & Bumble man, or a Kiehl's man, is sort of metrosexual in his ways, has made some money and knows all too well about fashion. Fashion was not Stephen's forte. He mostly dressed like a gym teacher, in wind pants and t-shirts—often of past theatre productions he'd done in college, like *Guys and Dolls* or *Waiting for Godot*. I thought that was cool and wanted theatre t-shirts of my own. This was the first man I'd ever dated who wore those kinds of things. It was a nice change from the Patagonia and khakis of the guys back home or in college.

"So!" I exclaimed and smiled anxiously. "Cool apartment."

I did not think his apartment was cool at all. The maroon carpet was the same texture as the one in our porch we had growing up—rough and harsh, uncomfortable if you fell. And all of the rooms were dimly lit, hiding the dirt that festered in every corner. The bathroom was filthy, with "I see you!" written in the bottom of the tub, smudged out of the dirt with an index finger. I didn't want to sit on the couch, picturing what it would reveal if that purple fluorescent light was put on it, unveiling the semen stains and other bodily fluids that you'd see on *20/20* or *Dateline* when they investigated hotels and their bedspreads. I sat in a folding chair that he had put out for me in front of a card table, which he kept stored in the closet for rehearsals like this.

"So I thought we could do this scene from a play I loved back in college," Stephen said.

"Great," I smiled, surreptitiously putting the plays I had in my lap back in my backpack.

"Only thing is, there's a part at the end where they have to make out each other. I mean, really maul each other. Do you have a problem with that?" He stared intensely. My face got hot.

"No, not at all, if it's not gratuitous," I lied.

I thought of the elongated pink sex-toy that my parents left out to dry on our bathroom sink when I was 10-years old--how I turned it over and over, trying to figure out what it was.

∧

The following day, after rehearsing in Stephen's apartment, he called me to rehearse again that night.

"Hey, you free today?" he asked.

"Yeah, totally," I said, as I sat on the front steps of my day job. I worked as office manager for a perfumery in Chelsea.

"What time?" I asked, feeling my heart flutter.

It was a Friday, and he suggested 10 p.m. I had never had a rehearsal on a Friday night…that, to me, was a date. Friday nights I usually spent trolling bars and downing Bud Lights with my college friends while looking for cute boys. But this was worth it. This was different, and perhaps part of my new life as a serious actress, where there was no distinction between a Friday night and a Monday morning. It was about the work and the craft.

Stephen showed up at 10, after he got off his waiter job. He worked in an old-style, upscale Italian restaurant in Midtown called Spollini's. He looked as though he'd been sweating. We read the script again and again, and had yet to rehearse the end of the scene where we make out. I was scared to do that, and my face got hot every time we read that part aloud and just looked at each other--for what seemed like hours--across the table. He didn't seem fazed by it, and I took that to mean that he was a more serious, and better, actor…those kinds of things were just part of the "craft"—his favorite word.

Since it was a Friday night, and to me something of a date, I had dressed sort of sexy for a rehearsal, with a DKNY spaghetti-strapped black tank top and a short jean skirt. I also wore my Dr. Scholl's that had silver glitter on the top strap across my feet, which made them sparkle like a disco ball when light hit them. We finished rehearsal at around midnight.

"So, what's new?" Stephen said and smiled, as he put the script away in his backpack.

"Well, it's my birthday," I said, which, indeed, it was: my 30th birthday. I kind of felt like a loser that on my birthday, and a big one like 30 no less, I was spending it alone with a random scene partner on a Friday night. But, in some ways I felt my nonchalance made me look sort of cool--as though I didn't care about birthdays, which was a total lie. (Full disclosure: my celebration was coming up the following weekend, when my friend Kara and I threw a joint b-day party at the local tavern, The Black Door, and invited 200 people on an E-vite)

"Tonight? Your 30th birthday is tonight?"

"Yeah, I know. Kinda major, right?" I said.

"Well, yeah! Holy shit. Wow. Well, what are we going to do about it? Do you like beer?"

HAH! DO I LIKE BEER?! I mean, I love beer, but that's another story. And hilarious to find someone who even has to ask me that, since half the time I spend trying to hide just how much I love alcohol, in general.

"Sure. I like beer," I said.

"Well, let's go out and get some."

I was ecstatic. He liked me, I thought. This was a date. I was not wrong about that. Good thing I was wearing my glitter shoes and a cute outfit, because I was all set to go out. Having to change to go to the bar would have made me look high-maintenance. Plus, he was wearing his usual wind pants and U2 concert t-shirt, so I didn't want to make him feel underdressed.

∧

The next day at work, all I could do was look forward to my next rehearsal with Stephen. We were supposed to meet at a church uptown by Columbia, which apparently had lots of open rooms with space to move and very little security.

"Are you sure we are allowed in here?" I asked warily, always being afraid to break the rules.

"Totally," Stephen said. "I've done it a million times."

I liked that he broke rules. It made him sexier.

I tried to act like I was having fun sneaking around the old church, opening and closing doors, when really I was petrified of being caught. I'm a rule follower to a fault. It never paid to break the rules in my house growing up.

"This room looks good," he said, walking in and putting down his backpack.

The room was huge, and it was on the top floor of the church, overlooking the Hudson, with small windows to look out, and gargoyle statuettes on either side of each window. I felt on top of the world, literally.

"Look at that. Baby crib and all the dolls," I said. "I think we're in some kind of nursery or baby room."

"Yeah," he said, picking up a Raggedy Ann doll and putting it down. "Well, the dolls can be our audience!"

He was so cute holding the dolls. I wondered what kind of father he'd make.

"Maybe we should start with some stretches and warm-ups," Stephen said.

"Sure. You lead," I laughed, having just pimped him out to be the leader. These games were always so embarrassing.

Stephen began to stretch in front of me, leading me through each move.

"Now reach all the way to the sky," he said. "On your tippy toes. Higher, Emma."

I didn't want to go any higher, as my shirt was already rising more than I wanted it to and my entire pasty, pale gut was revealed over my low-rise Paper Denim jeans.

"I'm trying!" I laughed, like a seventh grade girl, who pretends she can't kick the ball in gym class in front of the boy she likes.

"Now, one vertebra at a time, drop slowly to the floor, making your head the last body part to drop. And, as you do so, exhale and hum."

I tried to be serious with the rest of the exercise, because I didn't dare make him think I didn't take acting seriously. He was so serious about it. In fact, he was serious about everything.

We rehearsed the scene in "The Baby Room" (so we named it) several times, before we dared to attempt "the make-out scene."

"I mean, are you okay with doing the whole scene?" he asked.

At this point, I was dying to kiss him. And this was the perfect excuse.

"Yeah, if you are," I smiled, putting both hands into my front pockets and shrugging my shoulders.

"Totally," he smiled back. "Maybe, just to be more comfortable, we should turn the lights off the first time," he said. "Let's do the scene in the dark."

Oh my God…this was so romantic and hot. It was already dark outside, so we could see nothing but our shadows, the dolls' shadows, and the lights of New Jersey and New York outside the church.

We said the lines from the play, and with each line, I felt my heart thumping faster and faster, knowing the end of the scene, and the kiss, was near. I could hear him moving closer to me, as his wind pants crinkled with each step closer.

He got right in front of me. I could smell that he had eaten some sort of soup earlier. And I could smell his Speed Stick and Suave hair product. I wanted to taste the soup.

We finished our last line, and Stephen bent down to kiss me. His lips were full, really full, like Angelina Jolie's, and they sucked in my mouth, in a good way. I grabbed at his hips with both hands and pressed my body into his chest.

Then he pressed back and pressed his groin into mine. I put my hands into his pockets and could feel he was excited too. Good things come in big packages, and his was, well, big to say the least from what I could tell. Our breaths became heavy and our bodies hot. This was it, I thought. This was what New York was about--the skyline, following your passion, the actor. I was here, and I was in love.

Chapter 3

Only a year after Stephen and I broke up, I was in Woods Hole, jobless, and living alone on High Street with my 40-pound dog, a Vizsla named Dingo. I got Dingo at a rescue site when he was only 6 months old. Dingo was a great companion--always by my side, licking the water off the tub when I showered, sleeping in my bed each night, kissing my mental and physical wounds. But I missed cuddling with a person, so I figured I'd get back into the dating scene, and despite an initial hesitation, I willingly joined Match.com.

Match was a good distraction for me. I felt like I actually had friends and suitors, and I never had to leave the comfort of my couch, or my elastic band pants, even. I had a few email exchanges with potential in the works when I met my first real "Match." His name was Dave, or, as the tag on his profile said, "Scuplover323." No comment on the name, but nothing wrong with a fisherman. These were the types of guys I was finding on Match in Cape Cod. In New York, their profile names were things like, "TaxiNYC," or "Tribeca4U." In Cape Cod, I saw a lot of

"Boatman" or "Fisherman" or "Coast Guard."
Scuplover323 sent me email finally asking for a date:

> *Hey, Emma. What's up? Happy Friday.*
> *Just curious what you're*
> *up to this weekend, and if you'd want to*
> *grab a drink. --Dave*

Nice and simple. I liked that. Now, if I were going to play by "The Rules," I might have said I already had plans, since it was indeed already the weekend. Alas, I didn't have any plans. And being in a small town, he probably already knew that since everyone knows EVERYTHING in a small town. For example, "Hey, where were you running off to this morning at 8?" Or, "You looked like you were having fun at the 99 the other night."

I mean, you cannot go unnoticed…So I decided to write Dave back, minus any game, and tell him I was free, immediately:

> *Hey, Dave. Happy Friday to you too!*
> *Or should I say*

'TGIF?' I'd love to get together for a
drink. Want to grab
a beer at The Leeside tonight? Say
around eight? --Emma.

The email was out there in the universe. Now all I had to do was wait…and wonder why I had said "Happy TGIF!" Seriously!? I peeled off the sweatpants and decided to walk Dingo. Oh, and to finally take a shower. Maybe if I showered, it would put it out into the universe that I should being going on a date, and Dave would email me back, pronto. See, this is the problem with living in Woods Hole. You start saying things like, "put it out into the universe" and making karmic references way too often. I even had a conversation about feng shui, and I got into the habit of closing the toilet seat cover, because apparently that brings good fortune, or money. As I waited around checking maniacally checking my Inbox, the doorbell rang. It was Jeff. He was stopping by on his way home from work to see if I wanted to share a six-pack of Coronas. He held them up to eye level, smack in my face, when I opened the door.

"TGIF!" he exclaimed, tossing a lime in the air and catching it with one hand.

Just what I said! Jeff and I had an uncanny way of relating to one another. He was sort of like my solar twin, if there is such a thing.

"So, shall we? Mexican night? I can make fish tacos," Jeff said, trying to tempt me in the doorway.

"Oh…I'm sorry. You know how I love tacos and beer…but I can't tonight," I said. "I think I have a Match date."

"Already? Wow. That was fast. Didn't you join Match like--yesterday?" Jeff asked.

"Um, two weeks ago. That's a long time for the internet."

"Huh. What's his name?" he asked.

"Scuplover323…Either that, or Dave."

"I like 'Scup' better. I'm gonna call him that."

"Well, we may not even need to reference him after tonight," I said, "If it goes anything like my previous Match dates." I flipped open my cell phone to check the time for the tenth time that hour. I didn't want to be late.

"Huh. Well, want to pre-party?" He held the six-pack up to my eye level again.

"Maybe just one. Maybe I need a bit of a buzz to loosen up," I said.

Jeff set up shop in the kitchen, cutting limes, as I frantically tried on outfits for him, realizing I had the wardrobe of someone on *What Not To Wear.*

^

I stood in front of The Leeside for about five seconds and pulled out my cell phone. It read 7:55. Was I too early? When Dave emailed me back, he said to meet him "around eight." What does "around eight" mean exactly, anyway? I am always five minutes too early, and I didn't want to look over-eager, so I decided to get water at The Food Buoy, the local corner store, and peruse *US* magazine to waste some time. The bells hanging above The Food Buoy door jingled as I entered.

"Well, hello there, Emma. Hot date tonight?" Martin, the cashier, said.

"No!" I scowled back. "Okay, yeah. Wait, how can you tell? Do I have too much makeup on? Or is my perfume too heavy? Shit," I said, licking the back of my hand and pawing at my neck to remove the perfume.

"Eeeaasy, kitten," Martin said. "None of the above. Just noticed you don't look as *burdened* as usual, and I can see some skin."

I never thought I'd be described as "burdened," but I sort of like that it gave me some depth, a history. After all, I was the girl from New York. I needed some grit, some street cred.

"Yeah, well, I'm meeting a friend at the Leeside, just for a drink or two."

"Must be some friend," he said sarcastically. "Do I know him?"

Now, chances were that in this town he probably did.

"I don't know. His name's Dave?"

"Ah. That helps a lot. Dave…Dave…," he thought hard. "You mean Package Store Dave or Scuba Dave?"

Why did all these guys have prefixes on their names, I wondered. Like, there was a "Ricky Cold Cuts" and "Derby Dan."

"Um, maybe Scuba Dave?" I asked Martin, taking a wild guess. (I made the natural link between Scuba diving and Scup-lover).

"Cool. Good guy, Scuba Dave. He works on the Oceanus boat as a diver," Martin said.

Well, this was a good sign, I thought. At least he had a good rap around town, and Martin knew just about everyone, as The Food Buoy was the only place to get groceries and provisions in Woods Hole.

"Well, that's a relief," I said. "All right. I better go."

"You're not going to buy anything?"

"Oh, sorry. Um, maybe just this water. Thanks," I said.

"Maybe I'll come by and spy on you two later," Martin chuckled.

"Just don't embarrass me. See ya."

I headed to The Leeside and opened the door.

∧

I recognized Dave as I walked into the bar, looking past the five men decked in flannels and cargo pants hunched over cups of clam chowder and Fenway franks. I tried to walk with an air of confidence, upright, as my mother always told me.

"Stick your chest out and elongate that neck of yours," she always said. "Think Audrey Hepburn."

I tried to think Audrey, but I felt more like Richard Simmons. I was truly embarrassed and re-thinking the whole online dating thing. Then I spotted him. Thank God! He looked like his photo. Okay, so far, so good. "Dave?" I smiled, approaching the table. He stood up from his stool. Taller than I'd imagined. Nice. "Hey, Emma. It's you!" he smiled and stretched his hand out to shake. Good teeth, like Chicklets.

Seemed sort of formal to do a handshake, so I gave him an awkward one-armed hug, while his hand jabbed into my left rib.

"It's me," I laughed, pulling back from the hug and taking off my puffer jacket.

"What are you drinking? I'll get you another," I said. This was my effort of establishing off the bat that I was not expecting to be a kept woman. He did not have to pay for everything on the date (though, hey, let's be honest…it might be nice…). Jeff always told me women must at least "reach" for the wallet on a first date when the bill arrives, otherwise they look like a high-maintenance princess to the guy, and he might go running.

"Heineken," Dave said.

Nice, again. I loved guys who drink out of that green bottle. Somehow, it's sexier than the brown ones. I went to the bar and ordered a Heineken, pausing to think about what I wanted to drink. Now, if it were just me, or me and Jeff, for example, I would order a dirty martini, dry and straight up. But, since I am with a new date, who barely knows me, I want to appear sort of chill, laid-back, everyman's gal, etc…So I ordered a Bud Light. Guys don't want a martini drinker…or at least they THINK they don't. I'm what you call "Secret

High Maintenance," or SHM, as I call it. I appear to be all cool and casual, enjoying backwoods camping, shopping at TJ Maxx, getting ready in five minutes (all true)...BUT, the key here is that I also always choose to live in the nicest, posh neighborhood, like to be wined and dined and stay in nice hotels, and prefer First Class as a form of travel...But you'd never know that if you met me, and Dave--at least for now--would not know either.

I took the drinks to the table and met Dave, who was picking out songs on the juke box, next to the Buckhunter and Erotic Photo Hunt video game. I thought about challenging him to a game of Erotic Photo Hunt, naturally to show off my chops and break the ice, but thought better of us getting to know each other while discerning if the g-string was first up the girl's ass or simply laying flat on her cheek.

"I love these things," I said, maniacally flipping through songs on the jukebox.

"Yeah. They're great. What kind of music do you like?" Dave asked. "I know you have it on your Match profile, but I forget."

I hate talking about what music I like.

"Um, pretty much anything depressing and acoustic."

Yikes, that sounds so bad! And depressing. Another thing I learned from Jeff: guys like "happy girls." They don't want to take on anyone with baggage, issues, drama. They want "Light and Lively," like the yogurt.

"Sounds uplifting," Dave laughed.

"Yeah, well...I mean, no. I like all kinds of music. I just sometimes tend to listen to the more mellow, somber stuff. But, I mean, it's not like I'm depressed, or..."

I was falling fast down the rabbit hole.

"No, no! I know," he said, folding the outer corners of his cocktail napkin, looking down.

Did he know? I had to rescue this one.

"So, wait, what did you say you were doing today? Diving or?"

"Yeah, I had a scuba diving lesson after work. I'm training to work on a research vessel in Alaska in a few months."

Aha! It is Scuba Dave!

"Wow, cool. That sounds amazing. Do you like it, scuba diving?"

"Yeah, it's great. I mean, I'm out on the water all day, and I get to see all kinds of cool things, and we take trips all over the world. What else can you ask for?"

"Totally," I said smiling, thinking I could ask for a lot more...and not that. I mean, that sounds miserable floating around all the time with a bunch of guys who smell like fish and using yourself as shark chum.

"Did you go to school for that?" I asked.

"Yeah. I studied oceanography at University of Rhode Island," he said.

"Nice. Are you from Rhode Island?" I asked. I started peeling the wet label off my Bud Light bottle, a nervous habit.

"Nah, just wanted to be by the water and study the ocean. I'm going on a six month cruise up in Alaska this summer. I'm so stoked."

Well, there goes our future, I thought. What's the point of continuing? He's going to one with the whales up in Alaska. And I had to get used to this "be on the water" fascination that all these men I've met on the Cape have. I mean, it's like they're fish out of water, literally, who can't exist on land. I wondered if secretly they were Mermen, like Daryl Hannah in *Splash*, and perhaps they took long baths at night to spread out their fish tails in their bathtubs. Maybe I didn't get this water thing, because I'm from the Midwest, and the most water we saw was in the penny fountains at the mall or in the water slides at Cedar Point and Sea World.

"Where'd you go to school?" he asked.

"Northwestern," I said. "Go Wildcats!" I made a cat claw, raising my hand in the air, and immediately regretted it.

"Great school. What'd you study?"

"English…ya know, 'cause I wanted to set myself up for a job after graduation!"

"Seriously…must be kind of hard to figure out what you want to do with an English major," Dave said.

"Yeah, it's like, law school, or teaching, or reporting, or…God knows what. Living off your parents."

"Exactly. There's quite a few of those trust funders up here," he said.

"Really? I didn't notice," I said. "Seems so grungy and informal. Not like a bunch of rich kids."

"Yeah, but it's sort of that 'I want to look like I'm grungy and poor, but I drive a Saab and don't have to work and have a boat' kind of grunge. Don't let the long hair fool you."

"Totally," I laughed, wondering if Dave was bitter.

Dave and I chatted for the next hour or so, having a couple more beers, until we got to the good questions-- the ones that emerge after a few drinks when the filter is gone.

"So, why are you on Match anyway," he asked. "Seems like a girl like you could meet someone the regular way."

"Well, thanks, I guess," I said. "I don't know. I guess you could say I've been in a bit of a…funk of late, not getting out enough, and it seemed like an easy way to meet people without having to troll bars…or should I say 'the' bar, since there is only one in town."

"Huh. M' kay. Good reason," he said, flipping through the jukebox and landing on Guns N' Roses. "*Sweet Child of Mine*! I love that song."

"What about you? And how long have you been on it? Have you met a lot of people?" I threw all these questions out at once, as they came rolling off the tongue--what I really wanted to know.

"Well, I guess I've been on it for about two months now. Haven't really met too many women. Maybe six or seven?"

I pictured him having sex with these six or seven random women, all in the span of a month, who were possibly in The Leeside with us right now, giving me the evil eye. I started cringing inside and feeling like I might be in the presence of a player.

"Really? That's kind of a lot, no?" I replied.

"I guess. Not really. I don't know. None of them worked out, so…"

"Well did you try? I mean, did you, like, date these women, or…?" I asked.

"Not really."

"What's the really part?" I wouldn't let it go. Did he sleep with all of them is really wanted I wanted to know.

"Um…you're relentless, aren't you?" he said, taking a swig of his Heineken. I could almost see the red devil's horns emerging from his scalp, his eyes turning bright yellow.

"Sorry…I'll shut up."

"No, it's okay," he said. "I only slept with five of them," he said.

ONLY five!??! Ugh. I wanted to exit. I mean, that's a lot, since there are about only five single women left in this town in their 30s…unless… he totally shagged a 20-year-old. Pedophile. He probably likes Brazilian waxes, or "baby V's," too. I looked around the bar to see which women were giving me the stare-down. There was a blonde with frizzy, crimped hair in the corner, wearing a heinous turquoise sequined sweater, who was eyeing Dave. I imagined them having sex, with the sequins on.

"Huh," I said, trying to appear unfazed.

"How many guys have you met on Match?" he asked.

"Um, just you up here in Cape Cod. I did it in New York too for a bit, but rather unsuccessfully."

Then there was the redhead in the booth two down. She stared at me, picked up her bottle of Rolling Rock, stuck her tongue in it and took a voracious swig. It was a threat. She wanted back in with Dave, I thought. Hated to think where that tongue had been.

"Well would you say this is "a success?" he asked. I could tell he was nervous now.

"Um...yeah...not sure yet." I looked down. I knew it was over. So did Dave.

We hugged goodbye, this time with two arms, and he gave me a kiss on the cheek.

"Thanks. It was fun," I said.

"Yeah. Totally. So can I see you again?" he asked.

I didn't have the heart to tell him "no" right then and there. I'd wait to say it in email...the lame, chicken-ass way, referring to our "lack of chemistry." I hated myself right then.

"Yeah. Email me," I said.

"Okay. G'night, Emma. Nice to meet you."

I walked down Luscombe Avenue, wondering if I were being a prude for rejecting him merely because he slept with five girls in a month. Or maybe it was something else…or someone else…I didn't want to think about it and turned Ani DiFranco up on my iPod and walked home in the dark.

∧

The next morning, Jeff came to my house with bagels and coffee. It was our Saturday tradition: read the paper, eat bagels and process what happened on our Friday nights. Jeff never criticized me for eating bagels "the Christian Way," as Stephen had. Stephen hated that I ate the cucumber and tomato that were on my bagel and lox platter. He insisted they were just garnish. But Jeff and I were in agreement: the cukes were full-on food in our book, Christian or not.

"So…are you gonna keep me waiting? How was Scup?" Jeff smiled, revealing about eight poppy seeds stuck in his teeth.

"You look like a jack o' lantern," I laughed. "Want floss? I'm not sure I can talk to you like that."

"No, I'll get it out." He moved his tongue around, trying to un-wedge the seeds. "Better?"

"Better…but still not great."

"Whatever! Scup?"

"Okay, well…"

"It's over," he said, defeated.

"Wait, I didn't even say anything yet!"

"I know that 'well' start. It's done… What'd he do wrong? Was he wearing a floor length leather trench coat or Reebok high tops?"

"No. Actually, his looks weren't the problem. He's actually kind of hot," I said, tearing off a piece of bagel and throwing it to Dingo.

"Really? Why is he on Match then?"

"Excuse me, but I'm on Match. Did you forget?"

"No, I mean, whatever. So it wasn't the looks. What was it then? Did he have bad teeth or heinous breath?"

"No, it's just…he's had sex with a lot of girls. He seems like he might be a player."

"Hold it," Jeff said, smacking his bagel down on the plate and wiping his mouth, before he stepped onto his soap box. "What is 'a lot?' A lot for you? Or a lot for a normal person?"

"A lot for anyone," I yelled back defensively. Jeff knew about my prudish ways.

"You're just looking for a way out. How many women was it? Like 30 or 40?"

"Ew, gross! No! But I mean, like 10 in a month!" I exaggerated to make my point seem stronger. No luck. "Solid...Go, Scup," he said. "Emma, we are not in sixth grade. At least some of us aren't," he stared at me. "You are a 30-something, grown woman. People don't just go to second base anymore...they fuck...maybe even on the first date...maybe even not on a date."

"Do you have to say that word while I'm eating lox?" I asked.

"Yes. Fuck, fuck, fuck. That's what you should be doing. It's NORMAL."

"Well, I personally don't think so. I think it's gross to have sex with that many people in one month. I just do. Call me crazy."

"Um, I'm not the only one calling you crazy these days," he said.

"What is that supposed to mean?!"

"Nothing. Just, like, do you need an intervention maybe? You have been wearing those heart sweats for like two months, and I thought this Scup guy could at least get you out of those. I don't know. It seems like you don't want to be happy. And you're still not over Stephen." I tried to swallow immediately to conceal the tears that I felt emerging.

That was it. I was not totally over Stephen. But it had only been a year. I mean, isn't it supposed to take half the time that you were together to get over someone? (This number always changes, depending on if you're the one with the heart broken, or you are the one doling out the advice).

"I am over Stephen..." I said looking down, making origami with my napkin. "I just haven't met anyone I like yet," I lied.

"Fine. Whatever you say, Chastity. But, just make sure you get back online today. Don't use this one bad date with Playboy Scuba as an excuse for getting rid of your membership again."

"Thanks, Mom," I said. "Can I have the Styles section?"

"Here," he said. "'80s leggings are making a comeback. Why? Guys hate those."

"I'll add that to the list. What if you have good legs though?"

"Doesn't matter. Unless they are like pins, you're gonna look like a pig. No leggings," Jeff said. He grabbed the sports section, and we read comfortably in silence.

^

I met Jeff in the first week that I moved to Woods Hole. I was in The Food Buoy, buying my usual list, except this time I added at Stouffers frozen pepperoni French bread pizza.

"That better not be the last pizza," I heard coming from behind me, as I closed the freezer door.

"So good, right?!" I smiled, wondering if that response made me sound like I was from The Valley.

"Totally," Jeff said. I knew he got me. "I mean, how can you go wrong? They are like The Twin Cities of pepperoni pizza."

I laughed.

"You from the Midwest?" I asked, making conversation.

"No. Avon, Connecticut…but I lived in Ann Arbor, Michigan for a bit. My dad was a dean at the University of Michigan."

"Oh…I'm from Ohio! I went to Northwestern. Kind of like Michigan with Big Ten Football and all." I was about to raise my fist and make the "Go Wildcats!" claw but thought better of it.

"Nice. Go Wolverines!" We both laughed. Jeff was attractive. Tall--about 6'2, slender, with long legs, thick reddish/brown curly hair that had outgrown a style but was still short, and green eyes. He had some freckles too. I guessed he was some type of Irish.

"Are you Irish?" I asked.

"How'd you guess? Was it my Richie Cunningham looks, or the case of Fosters I'm carrying that gave it away?"

"I guess both," I said, looking around the store to see if anyone else saw us talking. Only Martin, the cashier, was there, and he was busy fervently scratching lotto tickets with extreme concentration.

"Yeah. Half Irish-Half Polish, I think. Who knows. I'm some kind of mutt," he joked.

"Too bad you didn't go to Notre Dame then," I said.

"Ugh. No thanks," he said. "The Fighting Irish? Not me. I'm more of a peaceful kind of guy."

"Oh, the Peaceful Irishman. Right, I guess that's why you're up here in Cape Cod. Making peace, smoking pot, growing your hair long…" I realized immediately that I might have sounded bitchy. I barely knew this guy, and I was poking fun at him. Why did I always do this? I overstepped my comfort bounds too soon, too often.

"Well, you're right about everything, except the smoking pot part. My drug of choice is beers and liquor. The only 'buds' I like are Budweiser's."

I found out that Jeff was actually a painter. He had been an art and religion major at Michigan, and he wanted to paint professionally. But, for now, he worked at a religious book publishers as a side gig to pay the bills.

I was relieved that Jeff wasn't turned off by my sarcasm and hadn't written me off. Actually, I think he liked my humor. He got me.

"So it looks like you're new in town," he said, tossing BBQ Utz potato chips into his basket. "Want to grab a drink?"

"How'd you know I was new in town?" I smiled.

"Um, maybe 'cause there are like five people who live here? And you kind of stand out. You're not wearing clogs, you have lip gloss on to come into town, and that Louis Vuitton tote bag is a dead giveaway."

I had gotten this bag as a present from my stepmother at Christmas. I loved it, but it was way beyond my budget. I tucked it under my arm pit.

"I guess I'm not doing so well at the blending in thing yet. I just moved here from New York."

"The City?"

"Yeah," I replied. I always just said, "I moved from New York," as opposed to saying I moved "from Manhattan." I hated when people said they lived in

"Manhattan" to people from outside the city. It just seems elitist to point out your more posh zip code. New York City is New York City--well, to people outside of it at least. Ask me this a year ago, and I would have zealously disagreed, cringing at the memories I had from looking at shitty apartments in Queens during a snowstorm.

"Just a wee bit of a change," Jeff said.

"Tell me about it. I went from eating New York Style pizza to Stouffers." I opened the fresh pastry cabinet and reached for a blueberry muffin and a cranberry scone.

"You did NOT just bust on Stouffers!" Jeff balked.

"You're right. Stouffers is no joke…"

"So want to grab a drink after you cook that up tonight? There's a bar in town called The Leeside."

I pretended I hadn't known this. One of the first things I did in this town was find where the local watering hole was. You never know when you're gonna need a cold one.

"Oh really? Okay, say 7:00?" I said.

"Sounds good."

"Okay. Well, I'll see you then!"

I wondered if it was a date…or a friend thing. Either way, I was happy to finally have a friend and someone besides Dingo to spend an evening with.

Chapter 4

I logged back into my Match.com the morning after my date with Scup. There was an email from him. Subject heading read: "Sorry."

> *Dear Emma:*
> *Hey. So great to meet you. I feel like at the end of the night*
> *I might have said something to make you upset. Sorry if that's*
> *the case. I would really like to see you again. Sincerely, Dave*

Well, that's nice, I thought. But since my next instinct was to go into the kitchen and grab a box of Bachman's sourdough pretzels and some jalapeno Pub Cheese for dip, I deduced I was not that into him. I certainly was not champing at the bit to write back or calling Jeff to ask exactly what I should say in response to his email. I let it lie. And continued my lie--that I was over Stephen. I told myself that everyone cries over exes, and it maybe it was the hangover from my date with Scup that made me vulnerable to tears. Pulling the geographic was good in terms of extricating myself from the daily misery of avoiding certain places, like all of New York with the exception of my apartment, but Woods Hole had not been good for my mental state as a whole. I still preferred to sit in front of *The Bachelor* for about 10 hours straight with a tub o' cheese than I did to actually get out there and date for myself.

And my life-avoidance reached further than my dating life and choice of waistband. It had seeped into my career, or lack thereof. At this point, I had no career. Trying to make a career as an actor in Cape Cod is, well, impossible, nor did I want to continue acting. I mean, sure, there was local community theater, like the Woods Hole Theatre Company and Cotuit Center for the Arts, but I was over that part of my life and wanted to start something new. But what? I mean, what skills did I have that made me actually employable, other than being able to memorize lines, muster up bad memories, connect to another person on stage…I mean, I was literally kind of useless. So I decided to go to a career counselor at the local community college.

As I drove into Cape Cod Community College's parking lot, I tried to plan out what I would say to this counselor. I was hoping that she would be insightful and be able to see that beyond my bare resume, of basically temping and waitressing--or should I say "culinary assistant"-- I certainly had some useful skills and a solid educational background to be able to make some suggestions as to my next move here.

"Come on in and sit down," he said--not she. The counselor's nameplate told me that his name was Mike Redding. Mike wore khaki Dockers, brown shoes with rubber, goober soles, and a blue oxford. He had his cell phone attached to his belt in a holster, like he was packing a weapon. Nice, Mike. Why do guys do that? If you're not part of the actual police force, I mean, really? So not attractive.

"So," Mike said, staring down at my resume, as he took a seat in his expensive Staples office chair with the black mesh back and adjustable height. (I only knew it was expensive because of my years as an administrative assistant. I often had to order supplies from the Staples catalogue and spent many hours perusing the various pages of the catalogue to pass the time until 5 o'clock).

"So, Emma, what are we here for today?" Mike asked. I hate when people use the proverbial "we" when they mean "me."

"Well, *we* are here to find out my next career step," I said.

"Great. That's my job, Emma!" He sounded like a car salesman, using my name too often to make the sale, something he learned in Sales 101.

"So, Emma, what are we thinking we want to do with our life? Any ideas?"

"Well, Mike, I don't know. I mean, I guess that's why I'm here. I sort of wanted you to decide for me what I should do."

Mike laughed.

"Now, Emma. I can't do that for you. But, I can make some suggestions after ascertaining your interests and skills."

"Great," I said. "Sounds like a plan." I noticed the picture of his golden retriever in a heart-shaped framed on his bookshelf. No wife and kids. I wondered if he was gay, heartbroken, or asexual. Couldn't tell yet.

"Well, we can start by having you sign up for the a career personality test. It sort of gets at what you think you are good at, your likes and dislikes, and it narrows down some career choices for you based on your responses."

"'Kay, sounds good. Can I take it now?" I asked.

"That was fast...Didn't have to twist your arm there," he chuckled and snorted at the same time. Poor Mike. I'm voting asexual now. "Well, at least we know one skill you have--efficiency!" Mike said, as he searched through his files for the test.

I laughed along with him to be nice.

"Here ya' go. Just bring it back in when you're finished. You can take it into that private office down the hall, if you like."

The test was comprehensive, asking me my likes and dislikes, such as:

1)   Do you prefer to work alone or with other people? (Alone)

2)   Are you more interested in the general idea than the details of its realization?
(Yes)

And, last, but of course my favorite:

3)   Do you feel involved when watching TV soaps? (Um, hello, have we met?)

So this was to determine what I should do next with my life---am I super-involved when I watch *Grey's Anatomy*? Well, yes, I am, especially when I see Stephen on an episode of *Ugly Betty* and it sends me into a tailspin.

I handed in my test to Mike, and he gathered I was a certain type that boiled down to a set of letters: ISTJ, which is an acronym for a personality type that translates into: Introverted, Sensing, Thinking and Judging. Sweet. Just what I wanted--to be judgmental and introverted. And I needed to take a test to figure this out? Thanks, Mike.

∧

I left Cape Cod Community College with my career and personality profile completed. Mike said that based on the results of the test, I would work well in a lab or in some type of scientific field. Since I had no real scientific background, other than the Introduction to Zoology I had taken as a General Ed requirement at Northwestern, and a variety of psychology classes I took when I was depressed and wanted answers, I might be hard-pressed to find a real lab job. But I figured it was worth a try. There was a hospital nearby, Cape Cod Hospital, and I knew they did research studies. Jeff once completed a Sleep Apnea Study at the Sleep Health Center there, when he went two months with insomnia. Turned out he didn't have Sleep Apnea--he was drinking too many lattes late at night, which kept him awake, tossing and turning. But, hey, he banged out some cash and helped the study, I think. Maybe I could use him as a job reference?

∧

The following day, I browsed through the online classifieds of the *Cape Cod Times* to see if the hospital was hiring. They always posted ads for something or other--a part-time RN or medical receptionist. And I was in luck. Bottom of the screen, highlighted in bold, a search result that read, "Research Assistant, Eating Disorders Unit." I clicked on the link. "Must have B.A. and statistics background." I wondered if one class in Zoology would suffice. We read about some statistics, like the number of bones in a turtle's rectum? Maybe it'd be sufficient. I circled the ad and felt like I had accomplished something for the day. Now I could take a break and watch *The View*. Sad how when you are unemployed, you are amazingly able to fill the day very well doing absolutely nothing. The phone rang. It was my mom.

"Hey, Mom."

"Emma? Is that you?"

Why did she always ask this, I wondered. I lived alone. And who the hell else would be answering my phone?

"Yep. It's me, Mom. How are you?"

"Oh," she laughed, acting surprised. "Great, I'm good. How are *you,* more importantly?"

My mom liked to play therapist with me. She constantly asked, "Well, how does that make you feel?"

It made me feel irritated.

"Um, I'm fine. Whatever," I said. Oh no, I'd opened a can of worms. Shit! Why couldn't I be one of those women who just says, "I'm fabulous!" every time someone asks? I always wear my problems on my sleeve, despite being an ISTJ personality type.

"Fine?! Just fine? Yeah? What do you mean by that?" she say prying.

"Nothing, Mom. Fine is fine. I'm fine!" I hated how I always ended up yelling at her. I was so unpleasant every time she called; she must think I have no social tact and did a bad job of raising me.

"Okay...well, so what's new?"

"Um, maybe found a job lead. Not sure."

"Really? Great. Doing what?" she said.

"Being a research assistant in eating disorders at the local hospital."

"Eating disorders, huh." I could hear alarm bells going off. "When did you become interested in those? Are you eating, Emma? Or maybe thinking about food a lot?"

"Seriously, Mom? No. It's a job opportunity, and that's it. I took a career test and they said that research was something I might be suited for."

"Huh. Well, great then," she chirped. "So you're settling into life there in Cape Cod?"

I knew that this really meant: are you never moving back to NYC and closer to home.

"Yeah, I don't know. I guess so."

"You guess so? What does that mean?"

"I *mean*, Mom, that I guess it's *fine*. Ugh, I have to go. Dingo needs to go out."

"You haven't walked him yet? What time did you get up?"

Truth be told, I got up at 10, but I was not about to tell her this.

"Seven, mom. I worked out, read the paper, did my resume, and time flew by."

I hoped karma was not a real thing, because the lies just kept coming.

"Oh! Good for you! Sounds productive."

"Yep."

"Okay, well give Dingo a hug from me," she said.

"Okay, I will. Thanks for calling, Mom."

"Wait, before you go…" she continued.

Here it was--the real reason for her call.

"What are your plans for the holidays? I was just thinking that---"

"Mom," I interrupted. "They are not for two months now. Why do you have to know today?"

I think she was unpacking the Christmas ornaments as we spoke.

"Can I tell you in a couple weeks?" I asked.

"Well, I just was thinking about whether or not I should plan on having you here. I mean, maybe I'll do something different this year," she said.

"What does that mean? What would you do?"

"Well…I guess now is as good a time as any to bring it up," she said. Her voice turned into a whisper.

"What? Bring what up?" I asked.

"Well…I've met someone. His name is Ron," she said.

I hated the name Ron. Sounds emasculated and like he wears a leather trench coat.

"Really? Wow. I had no idea. Well, good for you," I said. I think she was disappointed that I was not more interested or had a bigger reaction.

"Yep. I think this one could be a keeper," she exclaimed. I still said nothing. Waited for her to continue. "We have been seeing each other for about three weeks now, and he suggested that maybe I go down to Boca Raton with him for Thanksgiving to meet his children."

"Huh. Sounds serious. Wait, they live in Boca? How old are they?"

I hate Boca Raton. People who live there are too tan, or too old, or have had too much surgery.

"But, I mean, do you know much about him?" I asked. "It's only been three weeks. I don't want you running off to Florida with some psycho."

"Emma, honey. I'm a big girl and can take of myself. Besides, I Googled him. Didn't find anything sinister-- just some scores in a darts league he plays in on Wednesday nights."

It was weird for me that my mother had become so technologically savvy--doing things like Googling her dates. Note to self: Google Scuba Dave...

"Sounds like a winner, Mom. I know how you love to play darts."

"Oh, shut up. I'll throw a dart at you!" she laughed. "Be happy for me. I'm finally happy! After that *motherfucker*…sorry, I shouldn't call him that in front of you. He is still your father," she said.

She always did this--started to call my dad some expletive and then promptly apologized.

"Well, then I'm happy for you, Mom. Sounds like Ron is a nice guy." This statement was based on nothing other than my desire to wrap up the conversation so I could eat my pretzels and watch *The View*. It was another day of "Hot Topics," and I loved watching Whoopi get all flustered every time Elisabeth opened her Republican mouth.

"Well, let me know what you think about Thanksgiving when you figure stuff out. Do you think you'll be spending it with someone special up there? Is that why you're being so reticent?" she asked.

"No, Mom. Still single. Free as a bird." I turned the volume slightly up. Barbara Walters had just uttered something caustic.

"Well what about that Jeff character?" she asked.

Since when was he "a character," I wondered.

"We're just friends. Besides, he has a girlfriend," I lied.

"Well, you never know. Sometimes friends can be lovers." Isn't that some song that plays in the Rite Aid aisles?

I was silent.

"Okay, well, keep in touch. Remember, Emma, I love you." And the Academy Award for Most Dramatic Goodbye goes to....

"Me too. Love you too," I said. I dipped my pretzel in the tub o' organge-sherbet colored pub cheese and turned the TV up.

^

I decided to email Dave back and tell him that "the chemistry wasn't right." Translation: I am not attracted to you, you kind of scare me, and you've slept with too many skanks in town to count on one hand. But, hey, why be blunt about it and hurt his feelings? After emailing Dave, I checked my new matches. There were four, and two of them had a match percentage of 86 percent, meaning there was only a 14 percent chance we would not hit it off, according to the "Match" computer program. I first deleted match number one, based on his "header" or snag line to entice me to look at his profile: "2hot4u." It was like one of those terrible vanity license plates you'd find on a red sports car with tires that lit up. I deleted "2hot4u" immediately. Next, there was, "Down-to-earth seeks same." I mean, kind of boring, but at least he sounded normal. I clicked on his profile photo to read further. He was sort of cute, but he was wearing a hat in about 95 percent of his photos, meaning he's most likely bald an ashamed of it. The one photo in which he's not wearing a hat, he's very far away from the camera, and it's hard to tell. The hairline is definitely receding, but nothing that a little Rogaine can't fix. I decided to email him.

> *Dear Down-to-Earth,*
> *Hey. Read your profile, and I think we*
> *have some things in common.*
> *I just moved to Cape Cod from NYC as*
> *well. Do you like it?*
> *What do you do here? Anyway, just*
> *wanted to say hi. So...hi!*
> *Okay, well it'd be nice to hear back from*
> *you. --Emma*

I impulsively hit "send" and immediately regretted the text of the email. I sounded so pathetic! "Just wanted to say hi, so...hi?!" Ugh. Well, at least I sounded peppy and happy, so, if Jeff is right, that would elicit a positive reaction. Jeff must have sensed I was thinking of him, because the phone rang and it was him.

"So what's Whoopi bitching about today?" he asked. Jeff knew me too well.

"She's pissed at some author who said comedians don't make good parents."

"Robin Williams looked like a great father in *Mrs. Doubtfire*!"

"Yeah, I hear you...I'm now questioning Whoopi all together," I said. "So what are you up to tonight? It was Friday, which meant we were going out for TGIF drinks.

"Oh, let's see. Let me grab my appointment book," he joked. "Yeah, um...nothing. You?"

"You're looking at it," I said.

"I am not looking at anything; just my depressing cubicle. Want to grab a drink at The Captain Kidd say around 7?"

"Sure. Wait, I don't think I can wait that long to go out. I don't have anything else planned for today, other than a trip to Rite Aid." I was panicked. "Maybe can meet earlier, like at 5:05, when you get off work?"

"Mmmkay. See you then. 5:05. If I'm late, order me the usual.

^

With a slight hangover from drinking too many margaritas made with Cuervo--which is not even tequila, I learned--I got up early for my interview at the eating disorders unit. The principal investigator, a psychiatrist named Dr. Richard Manning, called me after receiving my resume and thought I might be a good fit for the job. I had fudged a bit on the statistics background, but how many stats were there going to be anyway? And wasn't there like a data person to do that?

I searched through my wardrobe to find something resembling a professional "career" outfit. My old corduroy blazer and oxford button-down with grey pants were about the only thing in there that looked somewhat acceptable. I had worn this for my Bounty commercial audition. I still had an unfortunate college-like wardrobe, composed mainly of GAP, Old Navy, and H&M gear, so looking sophisticated every day could be a bit of a struggle if I actually managed to get the job. I might need to buy a completely new wardrobe.

I arrived at Cape Cod Hospital's psychiatric research unit promptly at 10:20 a.m. for my 10:30 appointment. The front desk receptionist told me to wait in the waiting room before I could see Dr. Manning. I got self-conscious, seeing the other "patients" waiting with me and wanted to explain that I was there for a job interview, not therapy. I definitely did not look like I was there for an eating disorder, but there were other mental illness units on the floor as well--Depression, Bipolar and OCD. I picked up a squishy hand exerciser from the coffee table that was gray and in the shape of a miniature brain. The word "Remeron," some type of psychotropic medication, was printed on the side of it. I started squeezing it rapidly, in and out, to relieve some of my anxiety, then realized I might look like I was a patient there after all--not that there was anything wrong with that...

Dr. Manning came out of his office at 10:35 a.m. He was taller than I'd imagined, with a graying mustache and a thick head of salt and pepper gray hair. He wore glasses and was not traditionally handsome, but there was something attractive about him. I immediately looked to his left hand to see if he was married, to stop where my train of thought was leading.

"Hello, Emma?" he said, extending his hand.

I stood up, smoothing out my gray Old Navy pants to receive his handshake. No awkward one-armed hug this time around.

"Hi. Nice to meet you, Dr. Manning," I said, gathering my portfolio.

"Come on into my humble office," he smiled. He was humble indeed, as he had several impressive degrees hanging up on his walls, including an undergraduate degree from University of Chicago, and a graduate degree from Dartmouth Medical School.

"So. You get here all right in all this snow?" he said smiling.

"Yeah, no problem. I have four-wheel-drive," I said. "I learned you kind of have to when you move here."

"How long have you been here now?" he asked.

I pretended to count on my hands the number of months, when I really knew exactly how long I'd been there--as if the days were not scratched down in roman numerals on my wall, like in the movie *Shawshank Redemption*. Was Cape Cod like jail, I wondered?

"Let's see, about…four months?" I said.

"How do you like it so far?"

"Um, it's…good," I laughed, shuffling my feet around under my chair on the gray, wall-to-wall carpeting. I noticed Dr. Manning had several other of those brain hand squeezies on his desk.

"Good. So, I got your resume, and I'm definitely interested. Intrigued, really. So you were an actress before this?"

"Yes," I said. "But I do have a lot of administrative and data entry experience, from temping all those years. I also worked as an office manager for a perfumery."

"I see that. Well, those are all good skills to have that would be helpful in this job, as there is a lot of data entry. I should warn you: it's not the most glamorous position. We need someone who really has an eye for detail, is an independent and motivated worker, and who does not mind doing the grunt work of data entry and filing paperwork."

"No, that sounds great!" I said, really thinking that it sounded truly awful, but, hey, I needed a job, and this place looked as good as any.

"Well, so you don't have a statistics background?" Dr. Manning asked.

"Um, we did some stats in Zoology undergrad..." I smiled, trying to be cute and get away with the glaring lack of qualifications.

He laughed.

"I think we can deal with that. We do have a statistician. Just want someone who has a familiarity with math and how to read and report basic stats for psych journal articles and grant reports. But, having gone to Northwestern, I am sure you are a smart woman and would be able to pick it up after a few months."

"Thanks. I am sure I will."

"Well, let's see. So no plans on moving back to New York? We want a two year commitment here. Most of the other RA's, excuse me, research assistants, are here to get experience and apply to either medical school or Ph.D. programs in Clinical Psychology. Do you have any such plans?"

"I'm thinking about it," I said. In truth, I hadn't thought about it, but maybe this would be a new direction for me to move in. Maybe it was serendipity that I found this job and it led me to my next career? Perhaps the pieces were all falling into place, part of some big fated plan.

"Well this would be a great way to get that experience and to figure out if research is something you're truly interested in," Dr. Manning said. It seemed as though the tables might be turning in my favor, and he was actually looking for me to accept him, not the other way around.

"Definitely. That's what I was hoping," I said. "And I don't have any plans to return to New York. Or to acting, for that matter. I kind of feel like I've been there and done that."

"That's probably a nice feeling. I always wondered if people who try their hand in the arts and leave it for something more traditional truly yearn to go back."

"Not in my case. I feel like I got it out of my system, and I'm okay with putting it behind me."

"So did you do like Broadway, or...?"

I noticed that people were always so fascinated with the topic of my being an actress and wanted to know the details. It's a funny "job" to have, because everyone seems to be the expert, simply because they watch television and go to movies or plays. They think they know what it's like to be an actor and what it means to make it or not make it. And they're always asking you what's next and when you'll "make it." I mean, I never asked an accountant when he was going to get a promotion, or a lawyer when she was going to make partner, so why did everyone feel like they could ask me when I was going to be the next Julia Roberts or Patty Lupone?

"I never was on Broadway, no." I replied to Dr. Manning. "I did a few commercials, some day player roles on soaps, and mostly Off-Off Broadway."

"Now what is Off-Off Broadway?" he smiled.

"It's like third tier Broadway, if you're going to compare it to medical schools or hospital rankings."

"Aha, I get it. Well that's not so bad. Is it?"

"No, not really. I mean, I left for other reasons too," I said, thinking of Stephen's black hair and orange and brown backpack that he always carried. Was I seriously about to get into this with Dr. Manning?! I needed an intervention.

"Well that sound intriguing…Perhaps we can get to that another day…"

"So does that mean I have the job?"

"How about I give you a week to get settled and you'll start in two weeks?" he said.

"Perfect," I said. I thought of what I'd be doing to "get settled," and pictured myself putting in a few more days of watching *Ellen* and *The View*. I needed this job, pronto.

"Great. So do you have any other questions about the job," he asked.

"I think you've told me mostly about it. But, um, what's the salary?" I knew this was going to hit hard, in a bad way.

"Well, unfortunately the stipend is not very high, given that it's a research facility and most of our funding comes from grants."

I knew this was going to suck.

"The pay is $11/hour. Is that okay?" he squinted and tilted his head to the side, anticipating my quick exit.

"Sounds good," I said. "I just really want the experience."

"Great. I think you'll enjoy it here. There are a lot of other women your age and even some men!"

I looked out into the hallway, noticing the other RA's shuffling about and gathering in the meeting room for lunch with some drug reps and several tins of Italian food spread out.

"I see," I said.

"Drug lunch, every Wednesday. It's one of the perks," he said.

"Smells good."

"Well, let me know if you have any other questions, and I look forward to seeing you in a couple weeks. Just come in that Monday and report to me. I'll show you to your workspace."

"Terrific. Thanks, Dr. Manning. I'm really looking forward to it."

I stood up, shook his hand and walked out, holding my head high, feeling like my real life was about to start.

^

When I got home, I had an email from "Down-to-Earth" guy on Match.

> *Dear Emma:*
> *Thanks for the email. I'm kinda new to this stuff, so forgive me if I sound trite. I just moved to Cape Cod last month. Haven't met too many people so far, because I've been trapped at work. I'm a physician in internal medicine at the hospital. What about you? What's your story? I hope to hear back from you. --*
> *Greg*
> *P.S.-cute dog in the photo!*

Oh my God! Dr. Greg totally works at Cape Cod Hospital! I immediately envisioned us driving to work together, after having our Maple n' Brown Sugar

Quaker Oats instant breakfast and "a quickie." Or, maybe he was more of an Apples and Cinnamon guy? Oh, who cared…It'd be perfect. Then, I'd swing by his office on one of my breaks, closing the door behind me for a long and passionate kiss, before laughing and telling him I had to go before Dr. Manning noticed I was gone. Or, maybe we'd meet up in the on-call overnight shift closet, like they do on *Grey's Anatomy*, and we'd carry on our passionate lovemaking from the night before. I'd go back to work with that Heather Locklear tousled bed-head look, flushed in the face, with a Cheshire Cat grin. Oh, this was going to be good. I wrote back immediately.

> *Dear Greg:*
>
> *Hi again. So, maybe we have something in common besides moving to Cape Cod recently. I just accepted a job at the hospital as a research assistant. Cape Cod Hospital? Do you work there too? You know what they say about "dipping the pen in company ink!"*

Wait, delete that. Sick and wrong. I have boundary issues.

Dear Greg:

Hi again. So, maybe we have something in common besides moving to Cape Cod recently. I just accepted a job at the hospital as a research assistant. Cape Cod Hospital? Do you work there too? Maybe we could grab a bite to eat on one of our breaks. Look forward to hearing from you.--Emma

The waiting and incessant checking began. A doctor-- my mother would be so proud. As long as it was anyone besides Stephen, everyone I knew would be proud. Just then I pictured Stephen, his hazel eyes tearing up as we stared at each other for the last time when the elevator doors closed. He was wearing a white t-shirt that had a hole in the upper chest and a pair of black Addidas wind pants and the sneakers that I bought him for Christmas--navy blue suede Pumas. I wondered if he was still wearing those Pumas, but with his new girlfriend in tow. Maybe she'd buy him a replacement pair, as he was a hard and heavy walker, dragging his feet, and his shoes wore down quickly. I started to miss him again and went to my desk drawer to pull out the card the wrote me on Valentine's Day the year before we broke up. He had signed it "Forever Yours," which, in fact, is not true. Now that I am sitting here ultimately alone, up in the freaking woods, a semblance of Jodie Foster's animal-like character in *Nell,* I could see this line was bullshit. But, at the time, it meant everything to me. "Forever Yours." It was almost as good as a marriage proposal. Almost...

^

When I woke up the next morning, Dr. Greg had shot back an email. We planned to meet at Coffee Obsession, a local coffee spot on the corner of Water Street. He told me that he did, in fact, work at Cape Cod Hospital, and that he'd moved up here from New York as well, after completing his internship at Mt. Sinai. I was intrigued by all that we had in common before even having met. A repeat of *Oprah* was on the Oxygen channel when I turned it on to eat my cranberry and orange scone. She was talking about the book *Why Men Cheat.* The author suggested that it's the woman's fault. If a man does not get enough praise and attention, he said, and doesn't feel like he has won (using the analogy of their love of sports), then the man will look elsewhere to fulfill that need. Ugh, so typical and annoying that it's our fault. I constantly look for praise and attention, but I often find fulfillment in things like a bag Cheetos or a bottle of Kris pinot grigio. I don't need to find it in my co-worker, or that guy at The Food Buoy. Ew, just the passing thought of me getting down and dirty with Martin made me gag on my scone.

The phone rang and Dingo looked up from his dog bed with a look of foreshadowing doom. It was my mother calling from her cell. They say dogs have that sixth sense.

"Hey, mom," I said.

"Oh, Emma? Is that you?"

"Yeah, mom. Who else would it be? Didn't you try to call me? What's up?" I asked.

"Well, Ron and I decided to take a drive up to the country! And we're almost to the Bourne Bridge. I think we're a few miles from it…we're in Wareham," she said, emphasizing the "ham" part of Wareham--clearly a tourist pronunciation. They were only 25 minutes away.

"Really? Wow, so like…huh. What's your plan then?" I knew what it was but pretended otherwise.

"Well, we thought we'd stop by your house to say hello. That way, you can meet Ron. Then I thought we'd take you to lunch. That is, if you're not busy. Did you end up getting that food job?"

"What food job? I didn't apply to work at *Chili's,* mom. You mean the research assistant job in *eating disorders*?"

She laughed out loud at that one.

"Right, right! How'd it go?"

"Well, I got the job and start in a couple weeks."

"Oh! Good for you! Serendipity, Emma. Maybe your card is up this time. Things are going to work out for you, after all. I can feel it."

"Thanks. Um, so wait, are you like on your way to my house now?"

"Sure are! Ron has this amazing new GPS. We just plugged in your address, and this voice---" I cut her off mid-sentence. I could hear the auto voice telling them to make a right turn off the exit onto Route 28.

"All right. Cool! Wow. Okay, um, well I guess I'll see you soon," I said.

"Okay, baby. We'll see you in a jiffy!" She hung up.

I scurried around my house, picking up the refuse and clutter, or "spore" as my father liked to call it. Being a scientist, my father often referred to things by their scientific name, as opposed to speaking, well, English to me. For example, if I had a bruise, he'd refer to it as my "contusion." Or, when I'd complain about the heinous mole on my neck that I wanted removed immediately, he'd tell me not to be ashamed of my "nevus." The scientific way my father approached life was also how he approached parenting. He was very controlled and sterile. You know those developmental psychology experiments of nature vs. nuture, where they have one rhesus monkey raised by its natural mother and one raised with a wire monkey? Well, it felt like I was raised by the wire monkey--cold and inert. There were no hugs, no "I love yous," few feelings. We kept everything "light and lively," my dad liked to say. Just like Jeff said, men wanted to be around women who were light and funny, not full of problems and emotion. My father was this way. And, in turn, I became the exact opposite: needy, craving attention and warmth, clingy. And I chose to cling to whomever didn't like it. The more aloof the man, the more attractive he was to me. My mother was the same way, which is why she married my father. I wondered if Ron would be the exact opposite.

Scurrying to clean my apartment before my mom and Ron's arrival, I started maniaclly Febreezing the furniture and curtains to rid them of all Dingo smell. I lived on the first floor of a double-decker. A couple lived upstairs from me, but we rarely bumped into each other. They had a rusty blue Chevy that was always parked in the driveway. I assumed that they either never left the house, or they could walk to work. We hadn't really ever spoken, other than "hi" and "hey" by the mailbox. And I didn't hear them really, other than the subtle hum of the television at times, or when she put on heels, which was rare. I could hear her clomping around overhead but never actually saw her leave the house all dressed up. Maybe she was role-playing in a pair of stilettos, or maybe he was.

I stacked the *US* and *Lucky* magazines in the corner and put *The Atlantic* on top. This would make my mother feel better--that I was reading stories and an actual periodical, as opposed to some trash about a celebrity's weight gain or tragic breakup. I also decided to dust off my mother's picture from the bottom of my bookshelf and place it strategically out in the open in the living room. I knew she noticed things like this. And I made sure to put the one of my father hidden at the bottom of my sock drawer. The doorbell rang. "Helloooo--ah!" my mother gleamed, opening her arms wide for a hug. It was actually nice to see her. She looked pretty. Her silky brown hair had grown out a bit, and she was wearing it pulled back on either side with a pair of maroon combs. She wore a down vest and white, rabbit fur earmuffs. Guess this was her "country" outfit.

"Hi!" I said, reciprocating the hug. I looked over her shoulder and saw Ron smiling. He had small teeth. Looked like he grinded them at night.

"Hi there, Emma. I'm Ron," he said, extending his right hand, thin and spindly.

"Hey, Ron. Nice to meet you. I've heard a lot about you."

My mother looked at him and then at me, trying to register how we felt about each other. I could tell she really liked him, unlike the other two boyfriends I'd met since her breakup with my father. She seemed to have a glow about her this time around. Ron was dressed in brown corduroys, a tan turtleneck sweater, and a brown Carhartt hunting jacket. He must really like brown. He also had on a navy blue fisherman's cap and blonde-hair that was cut tightly underneath it. I wondered if he was in the military or was a conservative zealot.

"Well, come on in," I said. Dingo got up from his bed to greet them. He got to mid-calf and jumped up.

"Off!" I shouted. I so was not Cesar Millan from *The Dog Whisperer.*

"Oh, it's okay. We love you, Dingo," my mom said, crouching down to pet his little, white head. Dingo went over to Ron to sniff him out. I don't think he liked him, as he retreated to his dog bed immediately thereafter.

"Well, this is cozy!" my mom said. I noticed she was wearing a ring on her ring finger. It wasn't a diamond, which was a relief. It was some sort of flower-shape. I think she just liked looking "taken."

"Yeah, it's great up here," Ron chimed in.

"Thanks. Yeah, humble, but I like it." I walked into the kitchen to grab some vodka.

"Oh! I remember this photo," my mom said, reaching for the framed photo of her I had strategically put out. I knew she would.

"Yep. Good times," I said. "Can I get you guys anything? A drink? Coffee? A scone?"

"Oh, no scones for me! I'm trying to keep my girlish figure!" my mom said. Ron laughed.

"I think you are doing just fine with that," he said, giving her elbow a squeeze.

Okay, maybe they were kind of cute.

"So where should we take you for lunch? Are there any cute spots?" she said.

"Sure. There's this place in town called The Captain Kidd? They have like burgers and sandwiches."

"Sounds good to me," said Ron.

"Can I get a glass of wine there?" my mom asked. Since when was she a day drinker?

"Yeah. It's also a bar."

"Perfect!"

"Well maybe I'll get a martini," Ron said flirtatiously. Actually, maybe they were more annoying than cute.

^

The Captain Kidd was typically busy for a Friday afternoon lunch. Some people were there "on business," but I gathered from the amount of margaritas being churned out from the frozen margarita machine that most people were there for pleasure. That, and well, it's never too early to get started on a Friday, right? Isn't that where that TGIF term was derived? Or was it coined by Fridays restaurant--which, I must say, I have mourned the loss of its popularity. Seems like Fridays used to be found in almost any shopping plaza. The only one I knew of now was in Times Square in New York. That's where Stephen and I had one of our more momentous dates, where we decided to become "exclusive."

Stephen had just gotten off work at Spollini's, the Italian restaurant he worked at on 46th Street, otherwise known as "restaurant row." I met him outside the restaurant, and he still smelled a bit of Ragu, but he had noticeably cleaned up for our date, even sporting some gel in his hair. Granted, Stephen could never be too dressed up, as he always carried a North Face orange and gray backpack, with both straps on his shoulders. I think the double shoulder strap came back into style somewhere in our late-20s, because I know for certain in middle school that it was a definite fashion faux-pas to be double strapped. That was for nerds and wannabes. I think, to this day, my right shoulder might sit higher than my left, due to always bearing the brunt of my heavy textbooks on that one shoulder, carrying my purple L.L. Bean back pack with the silver reflector stripe and my initials monogrammed on the front pocket. I loved that backpack, until one day my BFF Samantha threw her lit cigarette out her front window, and it came back into the car from the rear window, landing on my LL Bean reflector and leaving a permanent cigarette hole.

"So, I was thinking we could grab some Sleds at Fridays," Stephen said, grabbing my hand outside Spollini's.

Sleds were the term we came up with to refer to potato skins that were super greasy and oblong shaped, and simply slid down the throat, like a sled.

"Sounds good to me. I always like sledding," I chirped back, loving every moment of him.

Whenever I was with Stephen, I never wanted to be anywhere else. And I always felt like New York was so much more exciting when I was with him. My life seemed more like a TV show, and I'd watch it from an outside point of view, complete with soundtrack, like I was watching an episode of *Felicity* on the WB network. Most of my songs were usually depressing, female acoustic, like Sinead O'Connor, and I'd take great strides with my long legs, swinging my arms back and forth, as I walked the streets of New York, feeling that much cooler and like someone was watching.

Stephen and I sat in the bar area of the Fridays, at a high-top table with a red-and-white checkered tabletop. The table was sticky, so I refrained from resting my forearms on it, and instead kept my hands in my lap, along with my napkin and utensils. I'm a bit of a germphobe, and the idea of putting my cutlery on the sticky, infested tabletop, where God only knows who was sitting there before me, repulsed me, even though it was the "polite" thing to do.

"So how was work?" I said. I flipped through the pages of the elaborate menu, chock full of colorful pictures of artery-clogging apps.

"Ah, the usual dildos there, making me run back and forth for drinks, instead of ordering them all in one round. I made pretty good money though, $300," Stephen said.

"Wow! That's like what I make in a week! Looks like you're treating!" I said, half-joking.

The funny thing is, I usually ended up paying more of the dinner bills than Stephen did. He did make more money than I, but I had the luxury of still being on my dad's dole if I needed it, and Stephen knew this. So, if I ran out of money at the end of the month when the rent was due, I simply had to call my dad, and a check for $1000 would arrive via FedEx free of guilt.

"Daddy send you another bailout?" Stephen would smile, as I tore open the FedEx. The part about it being free of guilt was not actually entirely true. I did have pangs of guilt when I'd open the check in front of

Stephen. And I was inclined to hide it, knowing that he would hold it against me and cash in on some of it later, claiming he didn't have the funds to pay for dinner, but he knew that I did. That money somehow seemed more expendable to him than his Spollini's money, as his was hard-earned, and mine was, well, a handout.

"So I've been meaning to talk to you about something," Stephen said, spreading extra sour cream over his sled.

"Oh yea?" I was nervous. He wouldn't dump me at a Fridays, would he?

"So are you, like, seeing anyone else?" he asked, putting the sled down on the side of his plate?

"Um, no…" I laughed, almost as if the question were entirely ridiculous. We'd been sleeping together for about 2 months now, spending every free moment together. But I played along. "Are you?"

"No, not at all!" he said, seeming relieved.

"Oh, good," I said, twirling my napkin around in my lap into a narrow, long tubeworm.

"Well I don't want you to…if that's okay with you," he smiled and started at me intensely with his green eyes.

"Fine by me," I smiled. "Me too…I mean, I don't want you to see other people, also." Now, granted, I thought this was a given by now, but apparently Stephen was one of those guys I'd heard of that like to have the "exclusivity" talk. I never understood that. If I was sleeping with someone, it was like I was mating them for life. I was kind of a bear in that way. Maybe I'd fare better in the wilderness, I thought.

"Great. So we're exclusive," he said, slapping a label on the relationship.

"Yes, we're exclusive," I said, moving my potato skin around on the plate, fearful of looking at him, to show how excited I was by our relationship moving to this new level.

My mom and friends would be proud. I was in a mature relationship now, and we were even mature enough to have the notorious "exclusive talk" that I'd read about in *Cosmopolitan* and *Glamour* advice columns.

My mom was not so proud of me now, as she sipped on her Shiraz in The Captain Kidd. We were sitting in a dark corner booth.

"Ew, I think Shiraz might have turned," she said, scrunching up her nose. "I suppose I could try one of those tasty looking margaritas that Ron has!"

Ron lowered his head to slurp from his straw. It made a gurgling sound, like when you got to the bottom of your McDonalds vanilla shake.

"I would highly recommend it," Ron smiled, licking his lips. I wondered why he asked for a salted rim if he was drinking it out of a straw, provided really only for mixing, as far as I was concerned. What kind of grown man, other than an invalid, drinks from a straw?

"So...?" my mom smiled, staring at me, as if I were to provide some monumental reply about the state of my life.

"So????" I smiled back, playing her little game.

"So, how are things here in Woods Hole? Are you glad you moved here?" she asked. I knew she wanted me to say no and return back to the Tristate area pronto. My mom was born and raised in New Jersey, raised us in New Jersey, and now continued to live in New Jersey. She didn't seem why anyone would want to live anywhere other than New Jersey.

"Yeah, I think I am. I mean, I have my moments," I said, recalling tossing the remote control at the TV and bursting into tears...or the Tourrettes-like outbreak I had leaving the Dunkin' Donuts drive-thru when they made it "light and sweet," as opposed to black, the way I like it.

"But, overall, I was just done with the city. I needed a break."

"From the city? Or from something else?" she said with a knowing-lead. I knew she meant Stephen. My mother wanted me to get engaged to Stephen, not so much because she liked him, but rather because she was desperately afraid that I'd end up a spinster. She got married right out of college, at 21, and to her, my turning 32 and being single was a recipe for disaster. I sometimes wonder if she was part of the reason for my break-up with Stephen. I think she scared him off at the annual summer barbecue, when she pulled him aside and offered to give him her mother's heirloom engagement ring to propose to me. I saw Stephen's face across the yard, gripping the sides of his plastic red and blue flag plate and trying not to choke on the macaroni salad.

"What do you mean by leaving for something else?" I partly scowled.

"Well I just wonder if you weren't running from your relationship with Stephen. And perhaps a little time away has done you some good, and now you can go back to New York. Maybe it wasn't New York that was bothering you," she said, slurping from Ron's straw. "Mmm, this sure is a yummy margarita," she smiled with her rose-stained lips.

I stared at the exit.

"Mom, I wasn't running from Stephen…entirely…I needed a change, and I couldn't see how I could make one living in New York for another 10 years."

"I know, honey. I think you did the right thing. I'm just saying maybe now you've had some time, and you might consider coming back. Ron and I would love to see more of you."

So I'd move back to my shit-box life to see more of slurpy-the-slurp Ron? Hah.

Just then I saw Scuba Dave across the room. He was eating a Chicken Roll-up with Ranch dressing, which I could see on the corners of his mouth, talking to some woman. I wondered if it was another one of his Match dates. I looked at myself in the reflection of my knife--a dull reflection, granted. I looked fine, but it could have been the dull cutlery talking.

"Mom, I'm gonna try it out here for a while. Besides, I just got this new job at the hospital, and I feel like I'm on a new career track, to be a clinical psychologist."

I simply wanted to do something meaningful with my life and focus on other people instead of myself. I felt like since I didn't have kids to take my mind off of me, I spent too many of my free hours spiraling and over-processing the details of my life, inevitably pathologizing most everything.

"So anyway...." I fiddled with the salt and peppershakers, sliding them around on the tabletop in figure eights. I noticed the salt was running low, and there were only hard rice pellets left in the dispenser. Looked like Sandy, the waitress, had not done her side-work the night before...or the night before that.

"So anyway," she replied. "Have you talked to Stephen, or emailed, or...?" She knew she was approaching rough waters and cautiously entered.

"Um, no, not really."

"What's the really part," she pried.

"Well he emailed me a few weeks ago just to check in and say hello. He heard I moved from Facebook."

"Aha. Well? So how was it?"

"The email? It was fine."

"And how are *you*...?" she continued to pry.

"I'm fine, mom, really. I think I'm over it."

"Well you were just so *in love* with him. I know it must still hurt." The salt trickled deeper inside my faintly healing wound.

"Yeah, well, not so much anymore," I said, looking down at the rice shaker.

"So! What are we ordering?" Ron said, changing the subject in desperation. "I think I'm gonna have the chicken wrap with ranch." Just like Scuba Dave. I looked over to Dave and we made eye contact. He timidly raised his right hand and waved hello. I waved back, wondering if I had maybe jumped to conclusions about him and should have given him another chance. The lunch lasted about an hour, during which time we covered topics such as Ron's family, my mother's newfound appreciation for spinning, and Ron's affinity for sports cars.

"You should have seen the look on his face when I went to drive the convertible!" my mom said. "He was white as a ghost!"

"Well if you didn't come so close to ripping the doors off on the side of the garage, then I'd have felt a bit better about it." I have to say, I sided with Ron on this one. My mother was a notoriously distracted driver. We had many a near-miss accidents when I was growing up. Perhaps the most frightening was when she was driving 85 miles per hour down the turnpike, trying to open a bag of Planters Peanuts. The silver, foil-like wrapper was sealed so tightly shut, almost childproof, that she had to pull and tear at it, using both hands...that left NO hands for the wheel when a Mack truck came peeling onto the pike off the ramp. We almost died, swerving lanes erratically to avoid a collision.

"Oh, you poo…" my mom said, slapping Ron lightly on the wrist followed by a squeeze. I could tell my mother really loved Ron, and I was happy for her. I watched the two of them interacting across the table. She was feeding him a peanut that she had de-shelled, a sign that she really loved him since she was willing to risk chipping her French manicure to do so.

**

My mother and Ron left Cape Cod later that afternoon. They were heading up to Maine to go outlet shopping at L.L. Bean and indulge in some fresh lobster. New Jersey wasn't exactly known for its crustaceans. I, on the other hand, came home to an email from Dr. Greg on my computer, asking if I wanted to grab dinner that night. I paused, wondering if I should follow *The Rules* and decline a last-minute date proposal. But, figuring it was between a date with Dr. Greg and a plate of nachos with Dingo and *Murder She Wrote*, I opted for a date, with our without the shameful smell of desperation.

The phone rang. It was Jeff.

"Hi," I sung.

"Well, aren't we chipper today? What happened? Did someone die?" Jeff said.

"No…but there might be a birth… the birth of my new relationship with Dr. Greg," I beamed into the phone.

"Huh, cool," Jeff said.

"That's all you have to say? Aren't you excited for me? I am actually going to shower and put on makeup and maybe get some action, not to mention a potential BF," I said.

"First off, why do women always assume that a date leads to a relationship? Maybe it's just a date. Did you ever think of that? Don't be desperate. Guys smell it a mile away."

"What crawled up your ass?" I asked.

"Ugh, nothing. Maybe it's this book on Tibetan monks that I've been editing all day. I feel guilty about my indulgent lifestyle. Maybe I should be more ascetic."

"Screw that. Have a martini; you'll feel better."

"Hah. You read my mind. Want to go grab one after I get out, at the usual, 5:05?"

"I would, but I don't want to be all liquored up when I meet Dr. Greg. He can find out I'm a lush later."

"Oh yeah, *Dr. Greg*," he said.

"Why are you so down on the doctor today? I thought you were encouraging me to get out there and date, and now I've finally met someone with potential."

"Why does he have potential? Because he's a doctor? You know, I hate that. It's like, if you're not a doctor or a lawyer, you're not really a professional; thereby making you just a flailing loser, who's throwing caution to the wind and has no future as a provider, or otherwise."

"Wow. You really are having a day today," I said.

"I'm sorry," Jeff said. "No, I'm happy for you…really. I think it's good. I just had a shitty day."

"Is this really all about the monks?" I asked.

"Well, that and…Jessica texted me. She wants to meet up later."

I hated Jessica and vice versa. She and Jeff dated for about six months. She wanted to marry him at first, but being the ultimate gold-digger, when she realized there was not much gold to dig, she left him high and dry and moved onto an older man, a banker at Goldman Sachs. I could tell she didn't like me the moment we met. She was threatened that Jeff and I were so close, and I think she was expecting to meet someone more homely. I was, in her opinion, a surprising threat. I think Jeff had described me to her, well…accurately…as a sweat suit-wearing, low-maintenance (he left out the secret high maintenance part), sort of Tomboy. So when I showed up with makeup, high-heeled boots and a low-cut sweater at The Leeside to meet them, Jessica looked surprised and somewhat annoyed with Jeff. But, truthfully, I think the competition made her like him more.

"Hi, I'm Jessica," she said, rising cautiously from her barstool. She was petite: 5'4, tan, long blonde hair, and a tight body. It was obvious she worked out and took great pains to perfect her package image. To me, she was more *Baywatch* than Cape Cod, but whatever floats Jeff's boat--just never knew he was into the 90210 look. It's funny, because I never noticed Jessica before, even in our small town, but once we met, I saw everywhere-- particularly on her daily jogs. She was always jogging. She was like Forrest Gump, but, hey, it worked. She looked good in those tight Sevens jeans and black tank top. I reached my two index fingers through my loopholes of my jeans and pulled them up over my one stomach roll as I sat down on my stool. The jeans were more comfortable that way.

"That's hot," Jeff laughed.

"Shut it and order me a drink," I said, looking over at Jessica, who was not amused by our comfortable banter.

"So Jeff told me you just moved from the city?" Jessica said.

"Yeah, long story."

"I heard it was a pretty bad breakup. Sorry. That sucks," she said, taking a ladylike sip of her Cosmo. The dangling heart from her silver Tiffany bracelet clinked the side of the martini glass, as if she was making a toast. I glared at Jeff for disclosing TMI (Too Much Information). He raised his eyebrows and shoulders feigning innocence.

"Um, the breakup wasn't so bad," I lied. "It's fine. It was more that I needed a change. The city can be too much after a while. I felt like I was always in line or always underground on the subway. I think I spent about 5 years in transit."

"Yeah, I go to the city a lot. My dad has an apartment in Manhattan." There it was again: the *Manhattan* specification. Strike two against Jessica. Strike one was bringing up my getting dumped in the first minute of our meeting.

"So, what are you guys up to tonight?" I asked, trying to step down and show Jessica I had no plans of infringing upon their couple-dome for the entire evening. She looked over at him, her blond hair flipping over her shoulder, and smiled.

"I dunno. What do you think, Shmoo?" she said to Jeff.

SHMOO!? As in the white, blobby cartoon character from the '80s that resembled Fluff with eyes? Didn't they JUST start dating too? I think it was a bit early for nicknames.

"Hm... whatever you want to do," he said, giving her a peck on the cheek.

OMG. I needed to extricate myself from the nausea, and fast. Since when did Jeff...or, excuse me, "Shmoo," lose his gonads and turn into Cape Cod's very own fine maple syrup?

"Well that sounds like a plan!" I balked. Jessica glared at me.

"We'll probably have a few here and head in," Jeff said. For some reason, I was extremely bothered by this. I didn't like the image of her in his house, sitting on my part of the sofa, but I knew I was just being possessive.

"Sounds good. I don't think it'll be a late one for me either," I said.

"Oh, are you meeting someone here after us?" Jessica asked, hopefully.

"Oh, um, no...I mean, I know people here, so...small town and all," I said bashfully looking around the bar, desperate to find a familiar face. "I think I see Ricky Cold Cuts over there. Might have one with him and call it a night."

Richard Carlson earned the nickname of "Ricky Cold Cuts," after working in the Stop N' Shop deli for several years. He sliced the deli meat perfectly into fine, thin slices, like an art. He loved deli meat.

"Really...?" Jeff smiled. "Didn't know you and Ricky Cold Cuts were tight."

"Well we got to talking the other day, and I think he's cool," I said, envisioning our last conversation over the deli counter. I was deciding between the Genoa Salami and the Turkey Pastrami, citing how "both have a nice flavor." Yeah, lots in common with Ricky.

"Hey, will you ask him if he's gonna get more of those buffalo wings, the spicy ones he had last week?" Jeff said.

"Yeah, I'll be sure to...first thing." I said.

Jessica was again not amused. I don't think she liked that Jeff ate wings from Stop N' Shop. I had a feeling she only shopped at the specialty stores and ate organic meat, or no meat at all.

"Do you know Ricky?" I asked Jessica.

"No. I don't eat cold cuts. I'm vegan," she said. UGH! Even worse than I expected...the ultimate in high-maintenance; vegans can't eat anything! No wonder she was so thin. How could Jeff even date a vegan? He was like the Meat Lover's Special in human form.

"That's how we met," Jessica continued, "at a book fair. Jeff was pushing the latest religious cookbook, *Buddhist Bites*, and I was trying to promote by book on vegan cooking, *Vociferous Vegans*. I just published it," she smiled, looking over at Jeff for approval. Isn't Vociferous Vegans kind of an oxymoron?

"It's really good," Jeff said. I think a lot of people these days are going Vegan. It should sell pretty well," he said.

"Are there like recipes and stuff?" I asked, noting that my face was scrunched up in disapproval. I immediately raised my eyebrows and smiled.

"Yeah, tons of them. I love cooking," she said. Total eating disorder, I thought. Makes the food but doesn't eat it. Red flag number one.

She annoyed me beyond belief. And I did begrudge her success. I couldn't then write her off as some dumb blonde. She was actually published, and I was circling ads in the local classifieds.

"Cooking's…fun." I said. We were running out of things to say, already.

"Well, I better get going. Ricky looks like he's waiting."

Jeff saw right through me. He knew she was not "a hit."

Jeff's relationship with Jessica ended about a year ago, and he never really mentioned her, but I knew he was not over it.

"So she texted you today?" I asked Jeff on the phone.

"Yeah. She said she has to talk to me about something. I have a feeling she's engaged to that old, rich douche-bag."

"Well why would she want to tell you that? It's not like you're friends, or that it ended well, or that you even dated her for that long to merit the need to inform you in person. This is suspect," I said.

"Maybe so…but I can't say I'm not curious," he said.

I knew Jeff was despondent when Jessica dumped him. She did it right before Valentine's Day, when Jeff had planned a weekend away at a B&B in Kennebunkport, Maine. He was super excited and even bought her this cheesy, but cute and sentimental, necklace with cupid throwing a dart while encapsulated in a heart on it. He never had the chance to give her the necklace and it's still in his top desk drawer (but who's snooping?!). I wish he'd throw it out.

"Where are you meeting?" I asked.

"At Natalie's at 8."

 Natalie's was one of the nicer restaurants in town, "known for its cocktails and innovative cuisine." A chef from New York had moved to Cape Cod and opened The Salty Tavern, and it took a year or so before the crowds caught on and ventured to try things like Tuna Tartare with wasabi and a soy glaze, or the Cucumber Cosmo, made with Hendriks gin and cucumber puree. These types of drinks were frightening and foreign to the Coors Light drinkers that usually romped around town at night.

"You guys having dinner?"

"Nah, just drinks. She likes the Cosmos there."

"The Cucumber one or the regular?"

"I didn't notice," Jeff said. Why do guys never notice these types of things?

"Well, I guess now I see why you're pissy…text me after the date. Let me know what she says."

"It's not a date, first of all. Secondly, won't you be out with the doctor-with-potential?"

"Yeah, but I can get a text."

"Don't have your phone on the table. I hate when girls do that."

"I won't. I'll text you from the bathroom. Thanks for the lecture, Emily Post," I said.

"Just sayin'," Jeff said. We both had a habit of saying this. It was one of our favorite phrases. It was the perfect retort and merited no response.

"All right. Well I gotta' get in the shower. I'm meeting Greg at 6," I said.

I felt bad for Jeff, but I was also sort of annoyed that he was seeing Jessica…and that she still got to him. I didn't like it. I hoped she was engaged.

∧

I don't know why I expected Greg to be wearing scrubs at the restaurant, but for some reason, I was surprised to see him in khaki brown instead of scrubs-colored-green. He looked cute. Very cute--taller than I'd expected, about 6'3, brown wavy hair that was neither too short, nor too long, and he had a sort of preppy, collegiate, Kennedy look. I liked what I saw and immediately became self-conscious. Was the lipstick I was wearing too pink? Should I not have ironed my hair straight and instead gone for a more bed-head, beach look? What would Jackie O' do in this scenario I wondered…so I smiled a large smile as soon as our eyes met across the restaurant.

"Emma," he said, flashing a very Ultra-Brite, white smile. So JFK. I loved.

"Hi there. Sorry I'm late," I said, knowing I wasn't late, but wondering how long he'd been waiting.

"Oh, no, you're not late. I was kind of nervous, so I got here a bit early," he smiled. I looked to see what he was drinking, a good indicator of his manhood. He was drinking a scotch on the rocks, a sign of a strong libido…(well, maybe I made that up in my head, but it sounded good and created nice visuals of things to come).

"Well nervous is good, I guess," I shrugged, taking a seat.

He handed me the drink list, and I opted for a Sauvignon Blanc, a nice Kennedy-esque drink. I imagined Caroline drinking some Sauv on a hot summer's day on the back patio by the pool in Hyannisport, watching Ed Schlossberg toss the football with the boys. Why did she marry him, anyway, I wondered. Whatever. Back to Greg.

"So have you started work on the Eating Disorders Unit yet?" Greg asked.

"Good memory! Yes, I actually started last week."

"So, how do you like it?"

"It's actually pretty cool. I mean, it's kind of a lot of grunt work and data entry that a monkey could do, but it's towards a good cause…the study, I mean."

"Definitely. Rich's studies are fantastic. He's published a lot."

"Who?" I asked, grabbing some popcorn from the red plastic basket.

"Dr. Manning, your boss?"

"Oh, sorry! I am not used to calling him Rich." I could feel a thin sliver of popcorn shell lodge into my molar. "Wait, you know him?"

"Sure. I mean, we all sort of know each other a bit. Plus, I've always had an interest in psychiatry, so I was familiar with his work during my psych residency."

I wasn't sure if his interest in psych was a bad or a good thing. It could go either way. The good way would be that he's sensitive and attune to emotions and feelings. The bad way could be that, well, he's a psycho. I decided to pry a bit further.

"Oh, you did a psych residency? Did you think about going into psych instead of internal medicine?"

"I thought about it, but, no offense, the people were kind of crazy--the doctors, not the patients, I mean." He reached for some popcorn, and I noticed how large his hands were with long fingers. They were almost as big as *Shrek*'s.

"Agreed," I said. "I hope I didn't scare you off when I said I was working on the unit."

"Well…" he smiled. I panicked. "Nah. Just kidding. You seem very sweet. And your profile on Match says "down-to-earth," so I figured I'd take your word for it." For a moment, I had forgotten we met online and thought we met in the hospital cafeteria. I guess that was part of my lengthy fantasy, where we were having hot sex standing up in the hospital broom closet. I liked the story of meeting at work instead and thought that that would be the one we'd tell all of our friends when they asked. Then I remembered Jeff and thought about his date with Jessica.

Dr. Greg and I had a nice dinner, and I ended the date "like a lady," (translation: not butt-wasted, keeping my clothes on, and only giving a hug and slight kiss at the door). We made plans to go out again during the week, because he had to go out of town to Tokyo for a conference on Syphilis.
∧

The following Monday I was late to work, because I popped into Stop N' Shop along the way to get my mandatory chocolate chip bagel with a smear of Tofutti on it. The line was all backed up. Ricky Coldcuts was hungover from a rough night of beer pong, he announced while at the meat shaver. I dashed off the elevator and onto the eating disorders unit, whereupon I found 20 audiocassettes awaiting transcription on my desk. The tapes were part of a longitudinal study we were doing on binge eating disorder among men, which often goes undiagnosed. I mean, I would have been terrible at diagnosing it myself, were I a therapist. Don't all men sort of binge on wings and pizza and beer until they're so full that they have to unbutton their pants while they watch TV? Maybe those are just the ones I've dated.

I think Dr. Manning had a history with it himself, and he now traveled around the country interviewing men on different college campuses about whether or not they were treated for their disorders, or even asked any questions leading up to an eating disorders diagnosis. The tapes on my desk were recordings of these interviews that I was to transcribe and then code, creating data. Each half hour interview took me about two hours to transcribe, so I knew I had my work cut out for me.

"Ugh, this is gonna be a rough one," I said putting down my Stop N' Shop bag and large French Vanilla coffee.

"What is?" Robin said. "Transcribing the tapes? It won't be bad."

Robin was one of the three other research assistants who worked on the eating disorders unit with me for Dr. Manning. We all planned to apply for Ph.D.'s in Clinical Psychology, but the difference between me and the other research assistants was that I generated the idea to go back to school about a month ago when I came upon this ad for the research job in the classifieds. They, on the other hand, had all majored in psychology in undergrad at their fabulous universities and planned on the Ph.D. since, well, they were like a fetus. I felt less driven and inherently insecure about both my intelligence and ambition every time I was around them. Robin, in particular, intimidated me.

"I mean, no, transcribing the tapes won't be terrible...I just mean it takes so long, ya know?" I said, looking for validation.

"No," Robin said curtly, searching through the manila folders in the filing cabinet. Robin was very terse and always had a way of making me feel like a blubbering idiot. Some therapist she'd be. I hoped she'd focus on the research side and avoid working with patients after she got her Ph.D.

"I don't know. Forget it," I said and plopped into my desk chair.

Robin was one of those girls, excuse me, *women*…(she would tear me a new one if she heard I referred to her as a girl, as she loved to say "feminism is a prerequisite for this job")…Robin was one of those women who was uber-smart and productive and kind of downright dorky, but for some reason, guys totally loved her, and she knew it. I think it *might* have had something to do with the fact that she had size triple-D knockers, and she batted the hell out of her eyelashes anytime a man was around, dropping all feminist ideology. But, whatever it was, she always had a boyfriend wrapped around her pale, stumpy finger. Robin was not the thinnest in the group, and thinness was, as you can imagine, a touchy subject among the eating disorder RAs. The other RAs on the floor, like the ones who worked in Depression and OCD, all had their own issues, such as who bathed in Purell to fend off germs and who missed a month of work with no excuse but wasn't fired. Weight, however, seemed to be an issue reserved for our part of the unit. Our group was very focused on body image and thinness, either being too thin or too fat. Robin erred on the side of being chubby, or shall we say, "cherubic," as she liked to say. I think she ate a lot to prove to the rest of society that you don't have to be thin to be successful and get a man. She would chow down at the drug rep lunches, showing the rest of then RAs just how confident she was about food and had no shame in indulging in seconds, sometimes thirds, of the Kung Pao Chicken brought by the Paxil sales reps.

"What!" Robin would say, grabbing a heaping portion of chicken, smiling at Andrew from Paxil.

"You sure can eat! Where does it all go?" Andrew returned the flirtation

Um, Andrew? She packs it all in her can. Can we say junk in the trunk?

"I just believe a woman needs to eat to feed her soul," Robin chimed back. "Don't you?" she said, looking around the room at the other RA's.

What soul is that, Robin? You are utterly awful, I thought, moving around the broccoli rabe on my plate. I looked over at Kimmie. She didn't ever touch the food that the drug reps brought.

Kimmie was another RA in our eating disorders group. She and Robin got along swimmingly. I mean, with a name like Kimmie, don't you always do everything *swimmingly*? I hate that name, but I actually liked

Kimmie. She was super-thin and tall--5'10, weighing in at 120 pounds, depending on what she had for dinner the night before and how much water she drank before her weigh in. The only reason I was able to know about her weight fluctuations was that we had a scale in the unit, on which the patients would be weighed before therapy sessions with Dr. Manning. Kimmie would remove her shoes each morning after dropping her brown, Cole Hahn leather tote bag off at her desk and head into my office, where the scale was located. She would remove any bulky items, such as a long, wool sweaters or heavy bangle bracelets and step on anxiously. She never commented afterward, or made any grunts or cheers for me to acknowledge. She simply stepped off silently, put her shoes back on, and returned to her office to eat her sesame bagel and drink her green tea. She would forget to move the weights back to starting position, so I could see how much she weighed, and, for some reason, it was habitual for me to check. Kimie obsessed about eating, and she had many food rituals. For example, she ate the same breakfast and lunch day-in and day-out: a dry sesame bagel for breakfast and a bag of Baked Lays (plain) with a Blueberry Yoplait for lunch. She would pick each sesame off the bagel, one by one, and place it on the wax paper to be thrown in the trash before eating it. She would never eat a bite that had sesames on it. I gathered this was because of the sesame oil that added calories, but it always struck me as odd that she wouldn't simply get a plain bagel and save herself the trouble. And she was definitely not a fan of my chocolate chip bagel choice. I once saw her scowl at it, making a grimace. I turned back around suddenly and she looked up at me ashamed.

"What?!" Kimmie said innocently as I stared at her, almost laughing.

"Did you just like throw mental darts at my bagel?" I asked.

"What are you talking about?" she said, picking off a sesame seed.

"When I turned back around your face was all evil and scrunched up, staring maliciously at my poor chocolate chip bagel."

"It was not!" she said. "I don't know HOW you can eat those," she continued. "I mean, all that chocolate first thing in the morning? Ugh."

"See? You do hate it!"

"Fine. Busted. I'm not a fan," she said.

The next day I bought Kimmie a chocolate chip bagel and left it on her desk as a joke. It was the first "present" I had given her. And though she despised having extra food around, and these bagels in particular, she wrapped it up in a napkin and carefully put it into her desk drawer. She kept it there, even when it was hard and stale.

The third Research Assistant was Claire. Claire had graduated Suma Cum Laudae from Princeton, had three cats, and, as far as I can tell, no life other than reading books. She left work every day, exactly at 5--kind of like Jeff--and walked home to her barn rental on Park Street to feed the cats. She then changed into pajamas, cooked herself some dinner and read until the lights went out for her to go to bed. I mean, to me, this was an abysmal lifestyle, similar to being incarcerated with pets allowed. But Claire seemed actually happier than most people I knew, including myself. It didn't seem to bother her at all that she was verging on spinsterhood. She just found the pleasure in little things, like her cat Pow-Pow learning to open the refrigerator door on his own. She was highly-depressing, but I must say I envied her simplicity and at times would have loved to trade the drama in my life for a little Pow Pow fun.

Not to say there was not drama on the unit--put four women, most of whom were in therapy, in the same office together 40 hours a week, and there is bound to be some drama. But the funny thing was, instead of just slamming doors or sending passive-aggressive emails, we would openly talk about it and communicate and share, something we learned in our individual therapy sessions outside of work, because, of course, we were all in therapy. We liked to call it "thera" for short, and no one would hold it against you on the unit if you left work for a solid two hours, as long as you were going to "thera." My therapist even worked at the hospital, so it was a hop, skip and a jump to get to his office.

"How was thera today?" Claire asked over lunch. We liked to sit on the floor of the office, on the soft green carpeting while eating. We didn't like to eat in the main lunch room with the other RAs from OCD and Depression. We instead chose to hide in our corner of the unit and talk amongst ourselves. The other RA's thought we were snobs.

"Thera was good," I told Claire, slurping some pumpkin soup. "Dr. Myers said he thinks the root of all of my problems are my father, and he suggested that I actually bring him in for a therapy session."

"Seriously? Wow, that would be intense. Would he even agree to anything like that?"

"Are you shitting me?! Of course not!" I laughed off the notion and shuttered to think of how awful it would feel to have my father sitting on the couch with me in Dr. Myers office.

"Did you have thera last night?" I asked Claire.

"Yeah. I got into a fight with her again. I mean, I feel like she has all this hostile feelings towards me and countertransference. It's like I remind her of her mother who took her off breast milk before she wanted to stop suckling."

"Wait, ew, did she tell you this, about the breast milk? How do you even know this?"

"Yes, I think she thinks we're somehow friends, or colleagues, since I work here in psych research. It's really inappropriate."

"Why don't you get rid of her?" I asked.

"I don't know. I guess I feel guilty and like I'm somehow responsible for her. I think it's part of me trying to reverse the shame I feel for ditching my mother in Baltimore when I know she needed me the most."

Heavy conversations like this were a natural occurrence. There were no secrets. And pathology was just accepted as the norm. If you didn't have a diagnosis, then your diagnosis was denial. Our openness with one another was actually pretty healthy, but...was it? Sometimes I wondered. Like, for example, did I really need to know that Robin had a terrible dream about me in which she stabbed me in the leg fifty times, and she translated this to mean that she was frustrated with me for entering the data incorrectly into the SPSS Statistical software program?

∧

Jeff never texted with an update about his "date" with Jessica, but we made plans to meet for drinks after work to process the whole deal. Kimmie decided to join us, as she and Jeff were also friends. They met three winters before I moved to Woods Hole at an open mic night at the The Captain Kidd. I reference "winters," as opposed to years, because that seems to be the protocol for talking about how long you've lived on the Cape. Summer doesn't count. That's the time when everyone visits, it's gorgeous, and it's the "season." Winter, however, is when it counts. That's when you officially become a "local." Being a local in Woods Hole does offer some benefits, such as a discount on breakfast at the local diner when you order the "local special:" two fried eggs, hash browns and vegetarian sausage. The waiters never check your zip code to verify, because they already know you if you're a local. I suppose you could get away with a few bucks off if you tried, but it's pretty apparent who lives here and who's visiting. There is something slower about the pace of a local than there is a transplant. For instance, walking down Water Street, the main street in Woods Hole, locals will often stop in front of Pie in the Sky for a long conversation about nothing of real importance, not noticing that the precious minutes are elapsing before they have to be somewhere else--which, unfortunately, is where my head is always at, somewhere else. Being in the present is so overrated (at least that's what I tell myself so I don't jump off the town bridge).

So Kimmie and Jeff sung a duet of Kenny Rogers' and Linda Rondstadt's *Islands in the Stream* at open mic night three winter's prior to my arrival, and they were instantly friends. He was sort of like her "beard" and kept people from wondering why she never hooked up or had a boyfriend. Everyone hooks up in the winter on the Cape--mostly, they say, to keep them warm. And there are *summer* girlfriends and *winter* girlfriends. The winter warmers are, as you might guess, definitely more homely and have a bit more cushion on them. Then, when the influx of summer girls from college occurs mid-June, the local men shed their winter warmers, like a dog sheds its coat, and they move onto a skinnier, more temporary gal. It's flat-out disconcerting, borderline disgusting. But, hey, what are you gonna do? People get cold.

Walking to The Leeside, I stopped off at The Food Buoy to pick up a pack of Trident Bubble gum and a raspberry seltzer water. I know gum is a disgusting habit, one that Jackie O' would never approve of (note to self: refrain from chewing around Dr. Greg), but I just loved chomping on it. Plus, it was a good way to keep myself from snacking, and my grey wind pants with the pink stripe were actually feeling a little loose these days, so I know it was working. God forbid I worked out and actually run, like Jessica. At least I was working out something, my mouth.

Martin was behind The Food Buoy register reading *In Touch* when I arrived. The bells on the door clanged behind me, which scared the store cat, Mittens.

"Sorry, Mittens!" I said, crouching down to pet his tail as he scurried to aisle three and hid by the Jiff and Fluff.

"Well, look who's here, Mittens! Miss Emma. Haven't seen you in a while. What's doing?" Martin asked, thumbing through the pages of celebrity gossip.

"Ah, the usual. Nothing really to report. What's new with you?" I said, feeling drawn to perhaps the Hershey with Almonds instead of the Trident gum. No, Emma. Not needed. Think Dr. Greg, not chocolate.

"Well, Jen might confront Angelina finally about stealing Brad," he said. "Other than that, not a whole lot." He paused. "You know, just been snowboarding a lot. I think I saw Scuba Dave out there boarding last week, as a matter of fact," he said. He was enticing me to take the bait.

"Really?"

"Yeah--so are you two..."

"No, it didn't really work out. We decided to be friends," I lied, whatever "friends" means. I guess waving across the bar at each other now constituted being "friends."

"Okay, phew," Martin said. "I didn't want to have to tell you that he was with Adrienne."

"Adrienne? Who's Adrienne?" I said.

"You know her. Muffins Adrienne? From the bakery?"
Muffins Adrienne? How unflattering a nickname. It
conjures up images of fat oozing over the sides of her
tight jeans with her thong sticking out like a whale's
tail.

"Oh, I didn't realize that was her name. Yeah. Well,
good for them," I said, placing the gum on the counter.
"You look a little sour grapes there, Emma. Does Dave
still have you hooked? That'll be a buck twenty-five,"
Martin said.

"Ew, not! Sorry to disappoint you. And, for the record,
he never had me hooked!"

The way I responded so angrily made me wonder if I
was indeed jealous or bothered. But why? Why did I
care if playboy-Dave hooked up with the muffin lady? I
didn't really. It's just--why did he like her when he
didn't like me? Wait, I had to remind myself: I didn't
like him first. Isn't it always this way? You distort
history so that you're the underdog victim in every
situation? Oh, wait, I think that's just me.

"Gosh, you really are feisty sometimes. That New
Yorker just jumps out of you every now and then,
unless you've had a few beers at The Leeside!"

"On my way now."

"Oh yeah? What's on for tonight? A little fooz ball or some pop-a-shot with Seignor Jeff?"

"Prob'ly. We'll see you over there later?"

"Most likely. Catch ya' on the far side."

"Okay, see ya', Martin."

I took my cell phone out to check the time. I hated to be late, ever. I was kind of like Big Ben, always aware of the time. My therapist told me that this contributed to my occasional anxiety, and he recommended that I stop wearing a watch. This was before I got a cell phone, of course. Now I just compulsively checked that. There was a text from

Dr. Greg:

Emma. Hope you are smiling today. I am smiling thinking of you. -Greg.

Awwwww, Greg! So cute! Wow, he really did have potential, beyond the "earning potential, or "EP," as Jessica and other goldiggers liked to call it.

Speaking of Jessica, Jeff was waiting outside.

"Hey, you," he said, giving me a hug. He smelled like Old Spice deodorant, the kind with the wolf on the stick. I took in a big whiff. I love the smell of men's deodorant--that, and new plastic, like when you first unwrap a toy or Barbie from the plastic Matel box. I used to chew on my Barbie's head because the smell was so good.

"Shall we?" I said, opening the front door of The Leeside.

"We shall. Thank you."

We headed to the back booth, by the dartboard. I surveyed the scene, and no one was really there yet, as it was of course only 5:05, and most people had the occupational decency to wait until after 4:59 to hit "shut down" on their computers. Not us. Jeff got a Jameson on the rocks, so I knew we were in for a long one, which wasn't so bad, even though it was technically 'a school night.'

"So? Jessica? How was it? Deets!" I said, carefully sipping at the rim of my dirty martini, neck extended like a giraffe, not lifting the glass.

"She's not engaged."

I didn't like the sound of where this was going. I hated her. Was she really coming back?

"Oh, really? What happened with the geezer? Did he give her the boot, or did the New York Stock Exchange tank, and she dumped him?"

"You really have to give her a break. She's not that bad."

"I have given her a chance, Jeff! Need I remind you that she left you high and dry for lack of EP?"

"Thanks for the reminder...No, I mean, I think she's changed. At least that's what she said."

"Oh, really? How is that? Now that she's a vegan, her soul is cleansed and she sees life in a new dairy-free light?"

"Kind of..." he smirked.

"I am so embarrassed for her," I said, shaking my head, hoping to God he wasn't going to say what he said next.

"I think we're going to give it another try."

"Wow."

"Wow? Is that all?"

"Well, what do you want me to say?" I looked up, and Kimmie was on her way in to join us. "Oh, perfect timing," I said.

"I don't know...maybe, "that's great?" or... "Are you happy?""

"Okay, that's great! Are you happy?"

"Ugh, forget it."

"No, seriously, I'm sorry." I felt embarrassed for myself now, and ashamed. What a shitty friend I was. Here was my best friend in the world who got his dream girl back. I should be happy for him, and instead I was being a royal bitch.

"It's okay. I know you two didn't hit it off exactly before, but she does like you. She asked about you and how you were doing," Jeff said.

I watched over Jeff's shoulder as Kimmie went up to the bar to order a glass of pinot grigio.

"Oh yeah? So what's her story now?" I said, envisioning Jessica's bony body running uphill past my house in her pink jogging shorts that had "PINK" slapped across her ass, like she was in the eighth grade.

"Well her book is selling quite well, actually, particularly in the Los Angeles market."

"Huh. Good for her." I hate her. Did I say that already?

"Yeah. I don't know…she said she felt like she made a mistake leaving things the way she did with me and she wants to give it another try."

"You said that. So what happened to Hugh Heffner?"

"We didn't get too far into it. She said something like they had nothing in common."

"Besides spending?"

"Be nice…"

"Okay. Sorry. I can't help it! Jeff! I hate this! I really have to take her back too now?" I whined.

"I'm afraid so! Cheers!" We clinked glasses." Kimmie plopped into the stool beside Jeff and gave him a hug.

"Nice outfit, Kimmie," I said, admiring her high-waisted Chanel black pants and emerald-colored ruffled tank. "I see you're embracing this year's gemstone colors!"

"Shut it," Kimmie said, reaching for the half-eaten basket of popcorn on the table. "So what are we discussing? Emma's Match dates or Jeff's depressing job?"

"Actually, Kimmie, we were just discussing the rekindled relationship of Jeff and Jessica."

"Stop it," Kimmie said. "For real?" She threw Jeff a disconcerted look. I knew we were friends for a reason.

"Yes, aren't we happy for him?" I said.

"Hi, are we in sixth grade?" Jeff said. "Yes, Kimmie. Jessica and I are going to go on a date. Whether we "rekindle our relationship" is up for debate, but we're going to meet for drinks, end of story."

I could tell Jeff was no longer amused and wanted to drop the conversation entirely.

"Okay, well, with that...moving on...to me and Dr. Greg," I said.

"Hold on," Kimmie said. "I didn't even get the chance to process the Jeff and Jess reuion and weigh in?"

"No," Jeff said. "I think we've covered it for tonight. Moving on."

"Ooohkay then! Well, so tell me about Dr. Greg."
Kimmie said.

"Well, it was good! And he just texted me something
really schmaltzy but so cute." I showed them the text
and pet the face of my cell phone.

"You love that crap," Jeff said.

"I know, he's pretty great. We're going out again this
week."

"Good. Maybe we can double date?!" Jeff said,

"I like it!" Kimmie said. "Maybe I can be the fifth
wheel!"

"Um, not," I said.

"Well, maybe someday we can double date," Jeff said,
trying to piss me off.

The way he said "someday" made me think he was
really serious about Jessica, as though there was going
to be a future with her, with like kids and vacations and
homes and stuff. Did I feel this way about Dr. Greg?
The three of us played a few rounds of darts and then
Jeff and I made our way over to the Pop-a-Shot mini-
basketball game about five drinks deep.

"G! That's PIG! I win!" I screamed, punching Jeff in
the arm.

"You totally cheated! That so didn't go in, until you
pushed it!"

"Did not!"

We were talking at a very high decibel, borderline screaming, at this point, but we didn't seem to notice or care.

"You owe me. Go get me another one, and give me some money for the Jukebox."

"Okay, secret-high-maintenance. Guess what's not a secret?" He handed me a roll of dollar bills.

The jukebox was perhaps my most favorite part of The Leeside. I loved being in control, and controlling the music was just one part of this. First off, it was a digital jukie, meaning I could download any song I wanted. But it was an extra dollar to download songs instead of just picking from the selection provided. I had to play my all-time favorite first: *Sweet Thing*, by Van Morrison. Jeff always rolled his eyes and feigned sleep when it came on. It was kind of a Debbie-Downer song in the middle of a party, but I loved it. And I always sat by myself in the corner, drifting off, imagining my bright, married future, or my shitty dark past--with Stephen. Jeff knew I liked this song, because Stephen played it for me on his guitar during the first few weeks of our relationship. Normally, I would cringe sitting awkwardly and listening to someone play guitar for me in a solo concert (totally awks…). But, with Stephen, as with all the other cliché things he did, I was smitten.

"Please tell me it's not coming on," Jeff said, walking across the bar.

"Sorry!" Just then, the first few chords of *Sweet Thing* played. I felt my eyes welling up…time to stop the martinis…but, I grabbed my refill from Jeff, and half of it spilled down my hand and onto my pants.

"I'm going to talk to Ricky," Jeff said. "I gotta give him some props for those buffalo wings." Jeff walked across the bar to meet up with Ricky. I looked around for Kimmie and saw her in the corner talking to the Pie in the Sky girls. They were the four women who worked in the bakery and always came to The Leeside when finished baking for the night. Not in the mood to talk wings with Ricky or popovers with Pie girls, I slid into the back booth, trying not to look like the drama queen that I actually was. I thought of Stephen's soft black hair and of his loft bed; I thought of how he'd fry me up steaks and Portobello mushrooms in his dank, blue kitchen, and we'd set the card table up with tea lights to make a romantic dinner at home; I thought about the sounds he'd made when we had sex in his loft bed; and I thought about how good he made me feel.

Then I did the unthinkable--I decided to put in the drunk call.

The phone rang two times, and I considered hanging up, but then a wave of bravado overcame me and I held on...waiting...would he pick up? Was he working at Spollinis? Shit, why did I call? My number was already logged into his phone as a missed call at this point, so I decided to leave a message:

> *Hey, Stephen. It's Emma...Um, just callin' to say hi! Random, I know...Um, maybe you're working...hope all is going well...Haven't talked to you in, like, forever. Um, anyway, nothing really to report here. I guess...I just miss you. So, yeah. There. I said it. I miss you. Anyway, I've had a few martinis, so please forgive me for this call when you get it in the morning. Ugh. Okay, anyway, call if you want to...no pressure though...Um...kay...Goodnight.*

For a few minutes, I felt good about the call. Yeah, maybe it was a good idea, I thought. Maybe he really wanted to call me, but he thought I hated him, rightfully so. Now I've opened the lines of communication again, and he can feel safe to call and apologize. I placed my cell phone on the tabletop so I would be sure to hear it when--and, more importantly, IF, he returned my call. I decided to have another martini while I endured my wait. Jeff was still up at the bar talking sports with Ricky Coldcuts. Jeff played ice hockey at Avon Old Farms in Farmington, Connecticut in high school and continued to be a huge sports fan, particularly of the Boston Bruins. He looked over at me and waved.

"Want another?" I mouthed to him, pointing down to my fresh, dirty martini with three olives.

"Um, I probably shouldn't...I am supposed to call Jessica later. She mentioned she might come by after her book signing that she's doing at the college."

"Fuck that! Don't be a pansy, Jeff. I need you. You're having another."

"Um...okay...?" he said.

I stumbled back over to my booth, almost twisting an ankle when it rolled harshly to the side in my clogs. "Effing clogs! I hate these! Why do I even have them on? Have I really given up or what?" I kicked my clogs off my feet and walked on the sticky brown wood floor to my booth.

Stephen had still not returned my call when I sat down to check my phone. It had been a good 10 minutes. I knew he had his cell on him at all times and checked it religiously, waiting for his "big break" call. About three sips into my martini, sitting alone in the booth, I realized something: he was not going to call. He hadn't up to this point. Why would he now? He never loved me, and I had to face facts. I was pathetic. Why was I even still thinking about this? Total loser. I deserve to be ignored.

I was crying when Jeff returned to the table.

"Oh no. What happened? We were having so much fun," Jeff said.

"I know. I'm fine, really," I said, wiping my Tammy-Faye Baker mascara from underneath my eyes.

"He is not thinking about you, and he never was. Stephen is a complete asshole, Emma. You are glad you aren't with him. It's definitely his loss, not yours." Jeff massaged my shoulders.

"I know. I just don't get it. Why didn't he love me? I gave him everything…all of me…Why?" I gulped from my martini glass and chewed on the green olive at the bottom.

"Well, look at you…"

We both broke into laughter, and I fell to the side on the red, leather booth. I could see chewed gum beneath the table, as my face rested on the seat.

"Let's get out of here," I said. I looked around for Kimmie but saw that she had pulled her usual duck out without saying goodbye. I hate that as a practice. Why do people think it's okay to just bail in silence? I like the long, stretched-out kind of goodbyes, full of peer pressure to stay!

"Wow, no love for The Leeside!" Jeff said. "Okay, where do you want to go? I have some beers at my place if you want to head over there."

"Sure. Sounds like a plan."

∧

When we got to Jeff's, I headed straight for his iPod to make the music at volume 100, like we were at a concert. We loved turning off all the lights, sitting on the couch, and just listening in the dark to music. Jeff and I had the same tastes in music, though I leaned towards depressing female acoustic at times, while he leaned towards country. Either way, both types of music were depressing and about relationships falling apart, so we were satisfied in any case.

I walked into Jeff's room to borrow a sweatshirt, because I still had my work outfit on. I went straight for his thick, Champion University of Michigan sweatshirt. Jeff's father gave it to him when he was accepted while still in high school, and it was old, soft and worn, with a hole in the right sleeve. It had history, and I always chose that sweatshirt when I went rifling through Jeff's closet for something to wear. As I passed his dresser on the way out of his room, I noticed that the cupid necklace he bought for Jessica was out. He had moved it from his top desk drawer. Was he going to give it to her again now, like some kind of fraternity pinning?

"Whatever," I mumbled, as my left hip hit the wood on the doorframe as I left his room. "Shit!" I said.

"What? You okay?" Jeff came running over with a giant knife in on hand and a lime wedge in the other.

"Yeah, the doorframe jumped out at me is all."

"You mean you're hammered and walked into it?"

"Sumthin' like that."

We lit some candles and turned the lights off while sipping on Corona's with lime. Jeff made fun of the way I stuck my tongue down the neck of the bottle every time I took a swig. I stared off across the room at his painting of the farm he had framed. Jeff was an Art History and Religion major, and he loved to paint. His work was Impressionistic. It was fun to look at when I was wasted, because it was even more blurry than it was.

"I love your paintings," I slurred.

"You do? Thanks." Jeff said.

"Yeah. You really have talent. I hope you know that."

"I just wish everyone else knew it too," he said. "Maybe then I could sell some of them, or get a showing in one of the galleries P-Town or Edgartown."

"Fuck those people who don't buy local—paint, I mean."

"Yeah, fuck 'em," he said, swigging back his beer. "I'm going to get another, want one?" Jeff said rising from the couch.

Led Zeppelin's *Stairway to Heaven* came on.

"Shut up! I love this song!" I grabbed Jeff's arm, pulling him back down. He fell closer to me on the couch than he was before. "Wait, you can't go get a beer now. You have to sit here and listen to this with me. It's so an eighth grade make-out song."

"It's a pretty good beat," he said.

As the song played and moved from slow to fast, I could feel the warmth from Jeff's leg get hotter next to mine. I started to feel a bit uncomfortable, uneasy, but in a good way. I wasn't sure if it was the song, the call to Stephen, or if I really actually wanted to make out with Jeff. But I didn't care. I wanted it, so I was going to go for it. I turned my head to the side to look at Jeff. He was looking across the room, and the flicker from the candle was making shadows on his face. He had grown some stubble. I thought about what it would be like to make out with him and stared at his body, wondering how it might feel on top of mine. Jeff then looked back at me. We didn't smile, for once. We just stared for what seemed like 10 minutes. And then it happened--we kissed. We started kissing passionately. He grabbed my face with both hands, strong hands that seemed unfamiliar to me. Jeff felt like a man to me now, not the boy next door, my best friend, or confidante. I leaned back on the couch, and he got on top of me, taking my wrists and putting them behind my head, taking control. I was immediately turned on and wanted more.

"Should we...?" I whispered breathing hard, trying not to kill the mood.

"Only if you want to," he said while kissing my neck. His lips felt soft and tickled. I giggled. "I want to. I've wanted to for a long time," he said.

"Me too," I said. We stared at each other up close and in the dark, him on top of me. It felt so unfamiliar and familiar at the same time. Then Jeff started to unbutton my jeans, and I unbuttoned his. Our motions and kissing got faster and more passionate. We clawed and pawed at each other, removing various articles of clothing. I took my hair out the elastic holding it back and let the curls hang down around my face.

"You're so beautiful," Jeff said.

"Stop," I said, embarrassed.

"No, you truly are, inside and out." He pushed my curls out of my face and pulled me towards him. We kissed some more, groped some more. I could feel he was excited, and it turned me on in ways I couldn't imagine. And then it happened. He was inside me. It was warm and wet and hot…and good…and nothing else in the world seemed to matter except for us.

∧

It was 7:55 a.m. when I looked across Jeff's living room at the clock on the cable box. My head felt like I'd been beaten with a baseball bat, and my mouth was so dry, as if I ate lint for dinner.

"Ugh…" I said, rolling off the couch onto the shaggy sherbet-orange carpet. Jeff remained on the couch, pants undone, shirt off. I stared as his chest and noticed that he had a lot of freckles. Did I even like freckles, I wondered? And why was his hair so red this morning? I never noticed that either.

Jeff opened his eyes and squinted. "Hey. You okay?" he asked. He was so thoughtful. Here he was, looking like he'd been hit by a bus, and he asked me if *I* was okay.

"Yeah, totally," I said. "Well, no, I feel like ass in a basket, but I have to get to work."

"Can't you just tell the ladies you had a binge last night? They'd understand."

"Jeff, we only treat binge eating disorders--not binge drinking disorders. There is no empathy for that one."

"Well, I tried," he said. "I have to get up anyway too. We have a staff meeting at 9."

I didn't say anything and walked into his room to retrieve my smoky black tank top and cardigan. It reeked of cigarettes from smoking in the alley next to The Kidd. I had a terrible habit of indulging in a smoke after a few...or like 20...drinks.

"You can wear my sweatshirt home if you want," he said.

"Um, no, I'm fine," I said. I didn't know how I felt about doing the drive of shame in Jeff's old Michigan sweatshirt. I didn't know how I felt about him, more importantly. And wearing his clothes home had BF/GF connotations. I wasn't sure we were ready for that yet.

For now, the sweatshirt could stay in his room…next to the cupid necklace for Jessica.

"Okay, I gotta go," I said, standing in the doorway. I contemplated kissing him goodbye, but it felt too awkward and forced in the light of day. "Sorry, just have to get home and let Dingo out."

"The old Dingo excuse. You can just say you want to go."

"Shut it, Jeff. It's not an excuse," I said and laughed that he called my bluff. "You are making me feel bad. Stop."

"Whatever, no worries. Just trying to make an awkward situation more awkward! Happy mornin' to you!" He lifted up a dirty margarita glass with a dried out lime on the bottom and a salted rim from the coffee table. "I'll call you later," he said.

∧

When I got to work, the other research assistants could smell something was up--or, maybe they could just smell me. I could still taste the olive juice from the dirty martins, despite brushing my teeth several times and wolfing down a chocolate chip bagel. I could also taste Jeff--and had flashbacks at my desk of him touching me. I was sort of turned on, but then felt immediate remorse, as in "What the fuck did I do?" kind of remorse. I mean, Jeff was my best friend, my soul mate, my kindred spirit. I didn't want to ruin that. He was my first and only real friend on the Cape. Everyone else here I felt couldn't be trusted. They were either too curious, hitting me with a slew of questions: Where do you live? Do you rent or own? How do you make a living with that job? What *do* you make? Or, they would outright ignore me, even if I'd spent hours talking to them at the bar the night before. I could have had an extensive conversation about someone's recovery from addiction, or their repressed childhood memories of an abusive parent one night, and the next day in the post office, I wouldn't even get a "hello." I never understood that. Was everyone just insecure? Or did I make a bad impression? It drove me nuts. Jeff, on the other hand, was always friendly, from the moment I met him. He was my go-to, "my person." And now we might have ruined that. Now he was my person without any pants on.

"Spill it," Kimmie said, stepping onto the scale. "What happened? With whom? When?"

"Um, hello to you too, Encyclopedia Brown. Are you on assignment?"

"Yeah, Investigation Emma," Kimmie said, shifting the calibrators on the scale from left to right. She wanted to be exact. I could see her moving the larger black weight to 100 pounds, but the smaller one barely moved past the 2-pound mark. I could tell by Kimmie's nose scrunch that she was not pleased. Maybe she had eaten a sesame seed by mistake and gained a pound. The underside ones can be hard to spot and sometimes sneak up on you.

"Jeff and I hooked up," I said, cutting right to the chase.

"SHUT UP!"

"For real."

I wasn't sure if she would be disappointed, since I thought she might be harboring a slight crush on me. She had recently split up with a woman from Provincetown, and every time she was single, she'd focus on me. Her invitations to the movies or to order Peking Palace Chinese at her house became more frequent. And she'd made me unsolicited mix-CDs, loaded with Ani Difranco, Tori Amos, Alanis Morrisette and Shawn Colvin songs. She loved to decorate the covers of her CDs with magazine images of women and painted lips, like those collages you'd make in middle school to hang on your corkboard.

Kimmie sat down on the green wall-to-wall carpeting in my office.

"So? How was it? Wait, are you like totally in love now?" she asked, grazing the tips of her fingers over the carpet and staring at the scale from afar.

"No. I mean, I don't know. I feel really confused," I said. I started twirling the hair around my index finger, a nervous habit.

"Wait, was it, like, bad?"

"What? The physical?" I thought of Jeff's unclothed body. He still had a hockey player's physique-- muscular thighs and a bubble butt from skating.

"No, the physical was actually really good...wait, I think." I tried to recall it through the foggy haze of many martinis. I remembered his touch being harder than I'd imagined given his sensitivity. And he was a good kisser, despite his thin upper lip. He always said he hated his upper lip, how he lost it when he smiled too wide in pictures.

"For all know," I continued, "I was a complete dead fish. Ew, I hate myself." I grabbed a Zoloft pen and started biting on the tip of it.

"You were not, I'm sure…" Kimmie said. "Besides, he loves you. You could do whatever you want, and he'd still love you."

"You think? But what about Jessica?" I asked.

"Seriously? Whatever. She's like a gross gold-digger having a crisis. She's going to leave his ass anyway, as soon as the next best thing with high earning potential comes along."

"Yeah…Well, not that I want to be sloppy seconds."

"You are hardly sloppy seconds, Emma! Jessica is, if anyone."

Kimmie grabbed the three ring binder containing all the data and the surveys that the male college undergrads filled out on our recent research trip to Boston University. We still had a lot of coding and data entry to do, but I was far too distracted to be productive. I looked out the window at the pond across from my office. Summer was coming, and I could see the algae forming a thin membrane across the top of it. I was told that by August, it would look as though it were a meadow instead of a pond because of the thick algae on top. I wondered if I'd still even be at the hospital in August. I felt the need to "pull a geographic" again. I hated dealing with confrontation, and my first instinct is always to run. But since the best reason, really, to move to the Cape is the summer weather, I figured I better stay for at least one tourist season. I hadn't had an opportunity to sample the fried clams at the seasonal Clam Shack or have frozen mudslides on the shells outside the Chartroom.

Kimmie went back into her own office, and I started to transcribe some male binge eating disorder tapes. My mind wandered away from the reports of eating four helpings of a Chinese food buffet to the drunk call I put into Stephen last night. I pulled out my cell phone from my purse to check and see if he'd texted me. He didn't. But there was a text from Dr. Greg:

Want to hang later?

Miss you.

I threw the phone down and looked around the room. I felt so secretive all of a sudden, like some sultry mistress who was juggling multiple men: Greg, Stephen and now Jeff. Maybe I should get a job at *The Bunny Ranch* in Nevada, I wondered. Big Daddy would pay me more than eleven bucks an hour. But, truthfully, Stephen wasn't really being juggled. He wasn't even in the picture.

Dingo was waiting for me by the door when I got home after work. He could sense I was stressed, because he walked around with his tail turned underneath him, forming a "C" shape. He always did this when he was nervous.

"It's okay, Dingo," I said, petting his sleek fur. "Mamma is just a little sad today." I grabbed him a bully stick to chew on, and he ran to his dog bed to indulge. The doorbell rang. It was Jeff.

"Hey…" I said.

"Um, hey again," he said with a sideways smile. I knew this smile. It was regret.

"Yeah, kinda hurting today, I have to say."

"Physically or mentally?" he asked. This is why I loved Jeff. He was evolved enough as a man to think about the emotional side of things…and to ask.

"Both, I guess. Want to come in?"

"Sure," he said.

We sat on the couch and stared at each other until we busted out laughing.

"That was pretty hectic last night," I said.

"Um…yeah."

"Are you totally regretting it and stressing?" I asked.

"No, not at all. It was fun." He was always good at making me feel better. He knew I was freaking out.

"Okay. You liar. Whatever… So what are you doing tonight?" I asked, thinking of Jessica.

"Um, not really sure. What are you doing?"

"Um, I don't know really."

I did think of going out with Greg, but this was not the time or place to mention that. I wondered if Jeff was concealing a date with Jessica as well. I grabbed the deck of cards on my coffee table and started maniacally shuffling them, like a Black Jack Dealer in Vegas. I flipped the cards over, starting a game of Solitaire and nonchalantly stepped up onto the elephant in the room. "So are you going to see Jessica again soon?" There it was. I put it out there, the acknowledgement of "another woman," thereby deeming the idea of an "us" as something that was either complicated or not happening.

"I don't know. I guess I will at some point," he said, grabbing my *People* off the coffee table and flipping idly through the pages. "Does anyone really still care about Fred Savage? Like he had his 10 minutes. Call it a day, Fred."

"I did love *Wonder Years*," I said. "I wanted to be Winnie."

"She was hot." He dropped the magazine and looked at me. I had nothing to say. "Well, I should probably get going. I just wanted to make sure you were okay with everything," he said.

"Yeah, totally. Wait, are you?" I asked, afraid to hear the answer.

"Yeah, it's not a big deal. Like I said, it was fun. If it happens again, then that's fine too," he said and smiled.

"Okay, good," I said. "Well I'll give you a call later. Maybe we can...nah, forget it."

"What?"

"I was going to say get after-work margaritas, but the thought of booze just made my stomach turn."

"Yeah, think I'm all set with that for at least a few days."

"Well, I'll give you a call," I said, closing the door behind him. Jeff drove off. Had we ruined our friendship forever?

Chapter 5

Sitting in Pie in the Sky for coffee the following day, I felt my phone vibrate as I was writing an email to Dr. Greg telling him how "I just didn't feel the chemistry was right." I couldn't handle juggling him and Jeff and had a complete mental shutdown. The phone number on my cell phone LCD screen read: 917-423-6879--it had no name. But I knew who it belonged to. How could I forget? I had dialed it for two years. It was Stephen. "Hello?"

"Emma..." Stephen said. His voice was gruff and masculine. I missed it.

"Yeah. Hi. Good to hear from you."

"Is it?"

"Shut up," I said, feeling shear panic and a need to poop. My bowels were always the first to go in anxious situations, especially when you add in coffee. "Hey, sorry about the drunk dial the other night. I heard a song on the jukebox and got all sentimental."

"*Sweet Thing*?"

He remembered.

"Yeah, the old go-to. Anyway, you didn't have to call me back," I said sheepishly.

"Now *you* shut up. I wanted to call you. I've been meaning to call you, actually... I miss you."

My stomach sunk, and I felt extremely nervous, like I was about to enter stage left during the climax of the play. I grabbed a brown paper napkin and started shredding it into little pieces, creating a pile large enough to layer the bottom of a hamster cage. Two children sitting at the round table next to me stared at me, shoving globs of blueberry muffin into their mouths.

"So how's New York?" I said, pretending not to hear the "I miss you."

"You mean, *Manhattan*?" He knew my humor, the right things to say, still. "It's, well, a bit lonely without you." He wasn't going to let this "miss you" theme drop. Not that I wanted to either, but I was scared to go down that road. It was too familiar, too risky. But maybe it was worth it--to smell his Suave shampoo again, to rest my head in that sweet spot between his shoulder blades and rub my fingers through the hair on his chest. I thought of "the baby room" from our first rehearsal.

"What? The ladies aren't knocking down your door these days?" Humor was my only defense.

"Hardly. But it wouldn't matter if they did. The only person I want knocking on my door lives in bum-fuck

Cape Cod." His cursing made him sexy, in a dirty trucker kind of way. "Where are you again?" he asked. "Woods Hole, a.k.a. Bum-fuck." We laughed and a long silence followed.

"Well how about a visit?" he said.

A *visit?* Holy crap! We were moving from a late-night drunk dial to an in-person visit? This was like the Acela Express train to heartbreak. I was freaking out: how long did I have to lose that 5 pounds? Why did I dye my hair red this winter? I looked like Little Orphan Annie--minus the cute red dress, add dog-walking pants.

" You want to visit? Here? Or...?"

"No, you come here," Stephen said. Of course, I thought; I come there. My eager anticipation was crashing and burning. I was put off. Why again was I the one making all the effort? It's amazing how the anger and resentment could bubble up so quickly. One moment we're laughing, the next I'm irritated. It's like when you're hungover, and the alcohol is still present in your system lurking just beneath the surface, and that first beer gets you drunk.

"I don't know. I have a lot going on with work and stuff," I said. Total lie. All I had going on at work was about 50 hours of transcription on male body dysmorphia.

"Well, I could come there?" he said. Now we're talking. Maybe he'd changed. He was flexible. He took the bait; I won the game; now I could submit. Was I really this childish? I thought about Stephen sitting in The Leeside and didn't like it. I wasn't ready for him to become part of this world yet, part of my safe haven.

"Actually, I am due for a trip to New York. Maybe I could swing it and come down there."

"Perf,' he said, mimicking the way I abbreviated words. I loved that he remembered the little things, like my in-the-know lexicon. "Next weekend? I'm not sure I can wait much longer than that."

"Wow, what's gotten into you?" I finally said. "I haven't heard from you in like, forever, and now you can't wait a week?" This all seemed very strange to me. Had he just been dumped by someone, I wondered? Or maybe there was a death in the family, or he realized he was never going to "make it" as an actor? My mind was racing.

"Sorry," he said.

"No, it's nice. I'm just giving you a hard time." I cleared the hamster pile off my table into my hand. I did have to wonder: why the sudden need to see me? I mean, this is what I'd always wished for, so why wasn't I running with it? Why was I ruining the moment with over-analysis and discussion? Oh, yeah, that's me.

"Sorry to ruin the moment," I said. "Ugh, I hate myself." So much for the cool act...

"No, I'm sorry, Emma. You have no reason to be sorry. I'm sorry for so many things. I've been meaning to tell you that for a long time now and just didn't have the balls to do it."

It was weird how even in a Hallmark moment, Stephen mentioned the word 'balls.' I wondered if they could create a card with something like, "You're the balls! Happy Birthday!" on it. Or, "It's Your Birthday! Celebrate Balls to the Wall!"

"But then you called, and, well, I guess I figured you couldn't hate me too much, so..."

"I hardly hate you, Stephen. Well, that's not true. I hated you for a while. But I think I'm over it now."

But was I over it? I wasn't sure. I definitely was not feeling hate--more like hope. I couldn't wait to see him. I couldn't wait to have make-up sex in his rickety loft bed, with or without the chance of a reconciliation. I just wanted to be with him again, in a primal way.

"Over it, or over me?"

"I'll see you next weekend," I said and laughed.

"Really? You'll come next weekend? Wow, holy shit," he said. "I didn't think it'd be this easy."

That made me feel like shit. A girl never likes being called "easy," in or out of the sack.

"I can't wait. I'll fry up some Portobello mushrooms and steaks, get a bottle of red wine. It'll be nice. Just like old times."

"Or maybe like *new* times?"

"Yes, that's better. New times," he said. "I like that."

I visualized the new times: taking trapeze lessons in the summer at the Chelsea Pier and skating figure eights in the winter at Wolman Rink in Central Park.

"Okay, I'll call you later in the week to finalize a plan," I said.

"You happy?" he asked.

Actually, I didn't really know. I thought I was happy, but it was so muddled with fear that it was hard to tell.

"Yeah. Are you?" Stephen always used to ask me if I was happy. Perhaps it was because he knew I was not. It wasn't until the one time I finally responded "No" that we broke up days later eating cereal.

"Totally; happier than I've been in a long time."

"Okay, I'll talk to you later," I said. "I mean, I'll *see* you later…"

I threw down my cell phone and looked around the coffee shop wondering if people noticed the wide smile across my face, one that hadn't been there in a long time. I took a sip of coffee and made a toast to myself: "To New Times."

∧

Chapter 6

"So, Stephen called you back?" Jeff asked, as we scooped nuts from the Trader Joe's raw food bins. "That was brave."

"Shut up! He's lucky I called him in the first place," I said, trying to believe my own bravado. "Do you take folic acid, or is it just for women who want to get preggers?"

"Um, no, and I don't know," he said, pushing his cart along the vitamin aisle. It had a broken wheel that kept turning forwards and backwards. "I hate these shitty carts. So what did you talk about?"

Jeff was inspecting the pistachio nuts. We had read that pistachios contained lots of miniscule worms, thereby ruining them as our nut-of-choice. "These look pretty clean. I'm going for it," he said, scooping a pound into a paper bag.

"Um, I dunno. We talked about a lot of things."

"Do you not want to talk about it?"

"No, I do. Why?"

"You just seem so reticent."

"No, I'm not. I'm just concentrating." I moved the tips of my fingers along the vitamin labels, like I was in the library searching for a book.

"Oh, okay, sorry. Didn't realize you were so serious about your vitamins."

I grabbed a huge bottle of chewable Vitamin C pills.

"Don't only like infants eat those? You sure you don't want the gummy kind?"

"I don't want to get scurvy!"

"So, what, you're not going to answer me?"

"No, I mean...he said he was sorry, which I guess is kind of huge."

"Really? Interesting," Jeff said. The wheels on his cart finally straightened out. He rolled off towards the butter and eggs.

"What is that supposed to mean?"

"So you accepted? That's it? You're friends again?"

"I don't know. I guess we're *friends*." I turned down the dairy aisle and grabbed a brick-like block of vegan orange cheese that read, '*Tastes just like cheddar*!'

"Does Jessica eat this stuff?" I asked.

Jeff didn't answer. "So I think I might go visit him...next weekend." I was scared to see his reaction. I knew it might not be good. Jeff detested Stephen and the way he'd treated me, despite having never met him.

He stopped his cart abruptly. "Are you serious?"

"Yeah, why?" I had a childish impulse to laugh, like when you're really uncomfortable while being punished. I thought back to the time my mother grabbed a horse crop that I had in the closet for my riding lessons and went to spank me. I had called her the "c-word" when she grounded me for having a party while she and my dad were out of town. I was crunched up in a ball at the corner of my bed, grabbing the pink comforter to protect me, and she stood over me, horse crop in hand, ready to strike, and just broke out into wild laughter… she laughed harder than I've ever see her laugh before. We both started laughing uncontrollably. She fell over on the bed, her chest heaving up and down, and that is one of the best memories I have of my mother, oddly enough. I missed her.

"Is that funny? Because I don't think it is," Jeff said, burning a hole into my blouse with his stare.

"What do you mean? Okay, Dad!" I said.

"Call me what you want. Somebody has to look after you, because, clearly, you can't do it yourself."

"What is that supposed to mean? I'm fine," I said, raising my voice. A lady looked up at me over her Breakstone's cottage cheese and lowered her leopard-framed reading glasses to the tip of her nose.

"It means that you are so quick to jump back into things with him, when he has no concern for you whatsoever.

He's using you, Emma. Again, it's always on his time. He calls, you run."

For a moment, it sounded like I was listening to my own internal narrative.

"That's not fair. I'm hardly running!"

"What do you call hopping the train to New York?"

"I don't know, Jeff. He said he's sorry. Maybe I'm curious. Maybe I want to…." I stopped myself and pushed my cart forward.

"What? Want to what?"

"See if we can make it work again!" I turned onto the frozen foods aisle and grabbed a box of Black Bean Boca burgers. Jeff's face was suddenly on the other side of the freezer door, defrosting it with his angry breath. He was like a dragon.

"Make it work?! Are you shitting me?!" Jeff yelled.

"What?" I wanted to laugh again.

"Nothing, Emma. I'm going to go check out. I need to get home. I'm meeting Jessica at 5."

"What? We're not having dinner? I thought we were barbecuing!"

I watched the back of Jeff's Black Dog t-shirt move farther away me. I guess I wasn't surprised by his reaction. But, in that moment, I really didn't care.

∧

Chapter 7

I didn't talk to Jeff for the next few days. It was lonely without him. I went to Kimmie's house for dinner on Monday, and we watched *The Bachelor*. I love that show, beyond a normal measure. Like, I never grow tired of determining "Who is there for the right reasons." I was also an avid participant in the online Fantasy Rose Ceremony game, where each week you try to guess which women are going to receive roses the following week. The winner of the fantasy game gets a trip to New York, complete with a cheesy horse-drawn carriage ride around the Central Park and a two-night stay at The Park Regency hotel. Maybe Stephen and I could hole up in the Regency if I won, I thought.

Stephen and I texted back and forth all week. He was being all cute, like when we first met, texting me things like, "Can't wait to hug you" and "Wish you were in my bed right now." I was literally jumping out of my clothes with eager anticipation for the visit. Wednesday night, I did laundry and took Dingo for a long walk on the beach. Dingo found a skate that had washed ashore, and he grabbed it by its weathered and sandy tail and paraded around the beach with it in his mouth.

Horrified, and fearing a potential parasite infection, I ran screaming after him, "Drop it!" He paid no mind and kept prancing around. I hated him in that instant, swearing profanities at him, and then felt unbelievably contrite and worried that I'd make a horrible mother who ends up on *48 Hours* or *Dateline* for "accidentally" driving her kids into a tree during a fit of rage.

On Thursday, Kimmie came over, so I could do a fashion show for her, and we could pick out my wardrobe for the Stephen weekend. I felt I had lost perspective since moving to Woods Hole, as clogs and long, flowey skirts started to look like an okay choice to wear out at night. I even started sporting a crystal necklace, like the kind that was popular with The Grateful Dead in the '80s. And let's not even get started with the Crocs... I needed an intervention.
"So what time is your train to New York?" Kimmie said, sliding the hangars across the bar in my closet. "This is heinous!"
She pulled out a bright yellow and pink flowered moo-moo that I had gotten at Wal-Mart when I first moved here. For some reason, I felt that I needed a "house outfit" at the regrettable time of purchase.

"Well, I took a half day, so I'll probably leave around noon. I'm taking the Acela out of Providence at 2:55."

"Some half-day. What can you get done in that time, check Facebook status updates?"

"Pretty much," I said.

"So you excited to see Stephen again? I mean, do you think he's changed at all?"

"It sounds like he's sorry, and he's had some time to think things over. I dunno. Maybe I'm being a naïve idiot--most likely--but I have to just find out for myself, ya know?"

Kimmie grabbed my Citizens jeans and threw them in my bag.

"What did Jeff think about it?" she asked.

"Not thrilled. We haven't talked since I told him."

"I don't blame him. You basically broke his heart," Kimmie said. I wondered if she was projecting her own feelings onto Jeff.

"That's totally false! He's the one who blew me off for dinner to meet with Jessica!"

"Whatever makes you feel better," Kimmie said. She threw my gray, Gap scarf on top a black tank top and tilted her head in judgment. "I just think it's a shame."

"What?"

"To throw what you two have away."

"I am not throwing anything away! God, we are just friends!" I screamed. Kimmie dropped the Burberry bag that was in her hand.

"What the fuck, Emma?"

"Sorry…I just wish *someone* would be a little supportive of me here. I mean, I'm finally getting what I want…what I think I want…and I'm terrified. Can I have little moral support? Please?"

"I'm sorry," Kimmie said, moving in for the hug. "I just want you to be careful. I care about you…and I care about Jeff, so it makes it hard for me."

"Have you talked to him?"

"No."

Friday finally arrived, and I was like a nervous cat about to take a trip: pupils dilated, almost panting. Every time I traveled, whether it be as far as Europe or as close at Maine, I entered this "cat mode." Growing up, I had a cat named Morsel, and every time we'd pack her in her carrier for road trips, she'd split her legs open wide, grabbing both sides of the cage, so we'd have to shove her in from behind, followed by a constant meow until the meds kicked in. Waiting in Providence station to board the Acela train to New York, I could have used some of those meds…wouldn't it be nice, I thought, if they had vending machines at train stations and airports that sold psychotropic medication? Like Klonipin and Xanax for those afraid to fly or leave the house?

The train was packed, as it always is on Fridays. I tried to strategically place myself before the Quiet Car door as it pulled into the station, keenly aware of my surroundings and standing far away from any obvious chatterboxes. There's nothing I hate more than making small talk an entire trip. And, even worse than that, being surrounded by two people making small talk an entire trip. Hard as I try to not eavesdrop, the voyeur in me can't help it, like I'm watching an episode of Real World.

∧

The train pulled into Penn Station at 5:40 p.m., and it was a relatively painless ride. In fact, I quite enjoyed eating a club car hot dog and chasing it down with a nip of Sutter Home chardonnay. (No judging…Nips are the way to go, even when you're not traveling). Exiting Penn Station, a wave of familiarity mixed with anger washed over me. You know how Carrie Bradshaw felt like she had a relationship with the city in Sex and the

City? Well, I'm not Carrie Bradshaw, by any stretch, but I did feel like I dated New York, and it was a painful, drawn-out breakup. I had avoided the city for just those reasons, because there were just too many memories, like those you have with a boyfriend, and, in the end, those memories were bad.

I walked up Seventh Avenue through the Fashion District and saw the Starbucks where I sat waiting for auditions on West 38th Street when it was cold out. As a struggling actor, you rarely get to wait inside the theatre or audition studio. You have to show up exactly at your call time, as though you'd just hopped off the train and in an outfit suitable for the role. More often than not, I'd wheel around a small suitcase with several changes of clothes in it each and every day, just in case I had a last minute casting call and needed to look the part. Casting agents always said, "Don't make it harder for the directors to imagine you in that role. If you're playing a period character, show up in a long skirt and shoe boots." Easier said than done. So I'd wheel around my luggage, in a mad dash from my day job, and change in a local coffee shop where I'd wait till my audition call time. I had one of these "green rooms" in every neighborhood--a safe haven where I knew there was a decent bathroom, sans homeless people, and a suitable place to sit undisturbed and keep warm. One of my particular faves was the GAP on 17th Street and Fifth Avenue. The bathroom was clean and very spacious, equipped with a huge handicapped stall that fit my luggage. Sometimes I'd even practice my monologue under my breath to myself in the bathroom. I'd look around me, mouthing the words, and I'm pretty sure there were times people thought I was homeless and crazy

It was early evening when I got to Stephen's apartment. An eerie feeling washed over me as I hit the door buzzer that I'd rung so many times over the course of our relationship. I thought back to our first acting class rehearsal and experienced some of the same nervousness--definite butterflies. I checked my reflection in the glass on the front door. I was wearing jeans, high-heeled black Marc Jacobs boots and a black tank top. So much for the Patagonia and clogs I'd be sporting in Cape Cod at this time. Stephen turned the corner with a huge smile on his face. He had come down the five flights to greet me, and he had pink tulips--my favorite--in his hands.

"Well aren't you a sight for sore eyes?" he said, giving me a giant bear hug. "Wow, it's so good to see you." He kept hugging. I could smell the skin on the back of his neck--a combination of Coast soap and Armani cologne. I had waited for this moment, this smell, forever.

"Yeah. Seems almost like it was yesterday," I said, taking the tulips. "Sweet. Thank you."

"I remembered," he said.

"You were always pretty good with the flowers," I said, recalling the last Valentine's Day we spent together when he sent a dozen red, long-stemmed roses to perfumery I was working at in Chelsea with the "Forever Yours" signed card.

"Well, shall we?" he said, grabbing my Vera Bradley duffle bag.

"After you."

The apartment looked basically the same, except it smelled of Lysol, instead of old garbage, and I could tell he'd attempted to spruce up the place. There were even a few "female" touches, like a light blue vase with dried hydrangeas on the coffee table and a few while pillar candles placed strategically around the apartment. There was even a lilac-scented Glade candle burning in the bathroom, and the tub was free of miscellaneous hairs and grime. I couldn't help but wonder if some other girl had been there, decorating the place, but I squashed any jealous or paranoid fantasies so as not to ruin the moment.

We walked back to his bedroom to put down my bag. There was no pretense that he'd be sleeping on the couch, or that we were taking things slow. It was just like it'd always been, fast and furious, passionate. Stephen put both of his hands on my shoulders and pushed me back onto the bed. We burst out laughing and started kissing. There was nothing left to say, only tons to do and explore, revisit. I missed the terrain of his body, the smell of his skin. It was all so familiar and felt so right. I couldn't believe how much I'd hated him over these last two years. It was as if nothing had happened. All the hatred and regret I experienced was tossed out his fifth floor widow onto Eighth Avenue and floated away. The only thing floating now was me.

^

"So how are you feeling about everything?" Stephen said, as we held hands walking around Columbus

Circle. It was spring, and the pink magnolia petals looked like giant blooms of cotton candy framing the entrance to the park.

"Good, really good." I squeezed his hand. It was thick and sweaty, full of anticipation.

"Me too. I'm glad you came. I was worried you would hang up on me when I called."

"Why? I had drunk dialed you just the night before!" I looked across at the Shwarma and Falafel street vendor to see if he was eavesdropping.

"I know, but I guess I just thought you hated me."

"I did," I said and laughed.

"Thanks."

"No, I did…but I don't anymore. Besides, isn't loving someone and hating someone basically the same thing?" I immediately wanted to recant saying the word "love." Was it too soon? Were all my cards on the table, an unsteady house waiting to fall?

"Are you saying you still love me?" he asked.

Just then, a horse-drawn carriage stopped right in front of us, and a man in a blue business suit got down on one knee in the carriage and proposed to his girlfriend. She accepted, shocked at the gesture, and put the glistening 2-carat ring on her finger. Granted, the proposal was dripping with Velveeta, and I personally couldn't think of a worse way to do it (actually, a football stadium scoreboard would be worse). But, it did seem crazily fortuitous at that exact moment in time. Stephen and I stood facing each other in front of the carriage. For a moment, I thought maybe he'd mirror the man and get down on one knee. I didn't know how to respond to whether or not I loved him, because, honestly, I wasn't sure. I had loved him for so long, that I thought of course the answer was 'yes.' I didn't want to lie, but I certainly wasn't ready to put myself out there to be hurt again.

"I still love you," Stephen said.

"Shut up." I couldn't look at him. I felt naked. Was he going to propose, I wondered? My mouth really dry, and it felt like I'd eaten cotton. It reminded me of the first time I smoked pot and was walking home on a first date with James Harding in high school. My mouth was so dry that I actually started sucking water droplets off the leaves that I picked from our front stoop hedges, hoping to hydrate and give a good French kiss. Now with Stephen, I hoped my lipstick wasn't crusting up, if in fact he was going to propose. No hedges around to hydrate either. Shit! I wanted to look my best. This was definitely not the outfit I'd imagined I'd be in when my prince charming proposed: jeans and Stephen's

Showboat t-shirt. No, this was all wrong. In my ideal scenario, I'd be in some couture Monique Lheullier champagne-colored gown with a pair of Christian Laboutin heels. Secondly, my hair would definitely be in a braided up-do, not greased back in a mango-colored chip clip. I guess the horse-drawn carriage had some Cinderella-esque qualities to it, but the fact that it wasn't ours sort of ruined that idea.

"Shut up?" Stephen said. "That's harsh! God, I tell you I love you, and that's the response I get?"

"No, I'm just kidding. That's nice that you love me, still...really," I said.

"Nice? That's all you have to say?" I loved how the tables had turned and Stephen was now the former me, begging for reassurance and smelling of desperation. Was that love, I wondered, that I wanted him to suffer?

"Well, for now," I said and smiled.

"As long as it's just for now," he said. "I'll put up with this B.S. for only so long!"

"Is that a threat?"

"Never. I never want to be separated again, Emma. I mean it."

I looked into his green eyes. I could see the tiny brown circles that surrounded his pupils, like the rings on a tree trunk, showing its age. He had matured, and I felt like he really meant what he said. As we continued to walk through the park, I could feel my emotional walls crumbling as our relationship gained strength. I knew I would have to give in if we were going to make this work. Stephen put his arm around my waist, and I put mine around his. We walked in tandem, our legs moving side by side, like the old days when we'd walk home from Murray's Bagels on Saturday mornings and get back into bed. The sound of Stephen's wind pants rubbing against each other with each stride was comforting, like a soothing lullaby. I felt like I had returned home.

Chapter 8

The weekend with Stephen flew by. He took both nights off from Spollini's, so we made steaks at home one night, and the other we went to Frank, our favorite Italian restaurant on 4th Street and Second Avenue. I always ordered the Ziti with Bolognese and a carafe of the Mezzacorrona wine. No messing around with glasses--straight for the carafe. After Frank, Stephen and I stopped for a drink at Bar Veloce on 11th Street and Second Avenue, a small, dimly lit bar with chrome stools and pink and black granite countertops. I ordered a Trimbach Pinot Gris, and Stephen got an A to Z Pinot Noir. He only drank reds. After about 10 minutes into the drink, I felt a hand on my shoulder from behind.

"Emma!? Is that you?" Melanie said, mouth agape.

"Hey, Mel!" I said, swiveling around on my barstool.

"You are alive! Oh my God! I miss *youuuuuu*!" She went in for the two-armed hug. Wait, did you like move to the woods or something?" Mel asked.

"Yeah, something like that. Cape Cod, to a place called Woods Hole." She looked confused. "I miss you guys too. How's the comedy group?"

"Ugh, it busted all up after you left. Timmy moved to Delaware to get an MFA in something or other, and

Jane got booted out. The rest of us are spread out on different teams now. Anyhoo! More importantly, how are *you*? What are you doing up there? Like Peace Corps or Noles or something?"

"Yeah, you know me, 'Ms. Noles!' Hardly. I don't know... Just needed a change of pace. Working in research, and…"

Mel's eyes glazed over at this point, so I stopped talking.

"How is it?" She looked as though she'd drank sour milk.

"It's good. Well, I mean, it has its ups and downs, but, for the most part, it's good. I just needed a break from the city and the acting grind."

"Some break. Couldn't you have done a spa day at like Bliss or something?" She laughed at her own joke and glanced over at Stephen for approval. "Is this your boyfriend?"

"Yes, I'm Stephen," he said, extending his hand.

Boyfriend? Did I hear that correctly?!

"Stephen? Wait, are you the Stephen—"

"Yes, that's him," I said, cutting her off, afraid of what was to follow.

"The Stephen that what?" he asked.

"Oh, nothing," Melanie said. She looked at me and winked to reassure me that she got my drift. "So do you live in Cape Cod too, Stephen?" Her attempt to play dumb was painful.

"No, not yet," he said.

"Not yet? Do you know something I don't?" I asked.

"Uh oh. Someone's stirred the pot, and I think her name starts with an 'M,'" Mel said and snorted. You know, she was never was that funny. I wondered why she ever chose a career in comedy, and why she was even got a place on our improv team. Then I remembered she was hooking up with the GM of the comedy club.

"Listen, I better split, before I really stir some shit! But it's great to see you, Em!" she said, going in for the second hug. No one calls me "Em." Now I remembered why we lost touch.

"Yeah, good to see you too. Take care, Mel. Tell everyone 'hi' for me."

"Will do! See ya'!" she said and bounced off down to the end of the bar.

"Not yet?" I reiterated to Stephen, hoping to start the conversation I had yet avoided: where this was going, our fate.

"I was just kidding! God, you seem terrified. Would it really be that bad? I thought you'd be happy."

"No, I just--" I thought about Jeff and pictured the three of us sitting on his couch listening to the iPod in the dark. Then I remembered hooking up with Jeff, what it felt like to have him touch me, strangely comfortable but sexy at the same time. I wanted more, but was that bad? Here I was with Stephen, the love of my life, and he was calling me his girlfriend. Some timing. "I didn't know that was even something you'd consider," I said.

"I mean, not really. I can't exactly be an actor there," Stephen said. "I don't know. Maybe I could come for summer training at The Wellfleet Harbor Actors Theater or something. Or maybe, I don't know, you could come back here?"

"To New York? Like to live?"

"Yeah, you know, to live, with me."

"Wait, you want me to move in with you?" I couldn't believe this. I had waited for him to ask me this question the entire two years we dated. Every time I broached the cohabitation subject, Stephen had countless reasons as to why he wanted to wait until we were "*both* ready." I gulped my Pinot Gris, motioning to the bartender for another.

"Well I guess I'd have to think about it."

"What's to think about? I mean, haven't you had a great weekend?" Stephen asked.

"Yeah, but it's only a weekend. And the first weekend back together at that, if that's what we even are--back together. Are we? Or...I'm so confused."

"You know as well as I do that this is good. We're good. We can make this work. I don't want to lose you again. Don't go back into the woods, Emma, please!" He laughed. I noticed he never really answered my question about our status.

"I don't live in the woods! Well, okay, yes, I guess I kind of do." I began to entertain the idea of heading back to Cape Cod and packing up, pulling a reverse geographic to move in with Stephen. What would Kimmie and Jeff say? Would they even care?

"Well, think about it," he said, lifting his wine glass for a toast.

"I already thought about it," I said, lifting my glass to his. "Let's do it."

"Really?" His eyes widened, like he an 8-year-old on Christmas morning when he spots his Star Wars figurines set up under the tree.

"Yeah, I'll pack up when I get back. I want to give us another try."

I couldn't believe I was saying this. Was I being an idiot? A hopeless romantic? I was actually moving in with Stephen! Holy Crap! Wait, maybe I did need some meds…was I being impulsive? I was notorious for impetuous moves and buys, like that time I came home with an iguana just because he looked lonely sitting my the pet store cash register. I wondered if it was okay to trust Stephen again. I couldn't bear another heartbreak. One was enough. But he truly seemed like he was being genuine and contrite. I felt I owed it to myself to give him, and "us," another chance. After all, I had spent almost every waking moment thinking about him and the sudden demise of our relationship…that is, until the last week when I hooked up with Jeff. Screw it, I thought. Carpe diem, live life to the fullest, jump and the net will appear…all those sayings…right? So long, Cape Cod! Hello, New York!

Chapter 9

"Okay, crack-baby," Robin said, lapping up her butternut squash soup while sitting on the office carpet Indian style. "What in the world are you moving back to New York for? Hasn't the therapy done anything for you these past few months?"

"Yeah, it has, and I think I'm in a better place now where I can actually go back and handle it better."

Kimmie said nothing. She just picked the sesame seeds off her bagel and threw them into the trash bin next to her chair.

"Did you tell Jeff yet?" Robin asked.

I looked over at Kimmie, wondering if she had told Robin about my hookup with Jeff, despite being sworn to secrecy. And if anyone knew about secrets, it was Kimmie. She looked back at me with an "I said nothing" blank stare.

"No, I haven't told Jeff yet."

"Why not?"

"I don't know. I guess I just got back late last night, so I haven't seen him yet."

"Well, I don't think he'll be too happy about it," Robin said and moved onto her side salad of mixed greens, blue cheese, walnuts and pears. "Actually, maybe now he won't care too much."

"What is that supposed to mean?" I asked.

"Robin, stop," Kimmie said.

"What?" I asked.

"Well, let's just say he didn't look too unhappy at The Leeside on Saturday night with Jessica while you were off romping in New York with Stephen," Robin said.

"Oh really? Was she all over him at the bar?" I tried to pretend this didn't irk me immensely. I am not sure whether it was jealousy I felt or just plain disgusted that Jeff would make such poor life choices.

"Um, try the reverse. *He* was all over *her*. I mean, like make-out central, in front of everyone. Even Ricky Coldcuts told them to get a room," Robin said.

"That's disgusting," I said, tossing the remainder of my hummus wrap into the trash.

"Well, I think you might have missed a good thing," she said.

"Watching the make-out? No thanks." I knew she actually meant Jeff but refused to indulge her. Why was Robin so up my grill now anyway? This was probably all motivated by her fear that I'd leave the research team with all the transcription and data entry on the binge eating study while the grant was due in less than two months.

"I'm going to go transcribe," I said, getting up from the floor and heading into my office. Kimmie continued to stare down at her bagel. She looked crestfallen. "Don't worry; I'll finish it all up before I tell Dr. Manning I'm leaving."

"You have to at least give two weeks' notice," Robin shouted after me.

"Thanks, boss."

While at my desk, I got a text from Jeff:

Hey. How was the weekend?

I wrote back immediately.

Hey. Good. Have a lot to tell you. Want to meet up after work? The usual?

Jeff:

Sorry. Can't. Have plans. Maybe tomorrow, lunch?

Me:

Lunch? Lame.

Jeff:

Screw you.

Me:

Hostile! Fine, lunch is fine. Tomorrow at Coffee Obsession? 12:30?

Jeff:

Sounds good. See you then.

∧

Coffee Obsession, better known as "Coffe O" was hopping at lunchtime. I looked around at the couches and wingback chairs and looked for Jeff. Then I spotted Ricky and Martin eating muffins at the counter with the newspapers. They were trying to hit on two women who were clearly tourists, decked out in Soft As a Grape "Woods Hole" t-shirts, with maps and gift bags littering their table. Ricky and Martin knew better than to try to hit on anyone local—you could never get away from them. I was struck by momentary nostalgia, feeling like I'd miss these guys, this scene, the familiar faces, the feel. Three scientists from the Woods Hole Oceanographic Institution sat next to me, wearing limulus t-shirts, talking about some new mollusk they'd discovered.

"Hey," Jeff said, sitting across from me. "You look sad. You okay?"

"Yeah, fine. Good. I'm actually not sad at all," I said, perking up in a fabricated sort of way.

"Good. What are you having? I'll order," he said, squinting to read the specials chalkboard above the cash register. "Sweet! They have the steak wrap."

Jeff always ate some kind of manly meat sandwich.

"Probably the veggie wrap with Swiss," I said. "And salt n' vinegar Cape Cod chips. When Jeff got back to the table, I could tell there was something different about him. His skin was brighter; he was dressed up--well, for Jeff--in a blue and white pinstriped oxford with khakis.

"So you have some news?" he asked. I wondered how he knew.

"What do you mean?"

"Um, your text? You said you had lots to talk about."

"Oh, sorry."

"Is everything okay?"

"Yeah, no, it's good, really good. Um…" Jeff looked at me. There was a pregnant pause. "I'm moving," I said. I looked to see how this bomb landed. I was surprised, to say the least. Jeff appeared unfazed, irritatingly so. I mean, this was huge! Perhaps the most huge of anything I'd told him since we met. I would have thought he'd have more of a reaction. Was it real, I wondered, or was he covering it up? Maybe he was just devastated by the news but didn't want to ruin it for me.

"To New York?" He popped a few chips into his mouth, an annoying gesture, like he was casually eating peanuts and talking about football at a 4th of July picnic.

"How did you know?" I asked, wondering if he had talked to Kimmie.

"Just figured it was going down that road."

"So what do you think?" I wasn't sure I really wanted an honest answer, since I'd already made up my mind, but I did want his approval. I desperately wanted his approval.

"Honestly, Emma? I think it's a terrible idea. But you know what? It doesn't matter what I think. It's your life, not mine, and you're going to do what you're going to do," he said. He threw his scrunched up napkin down onto the table, like some sort of punctuation.

"Can you not?"

"Sorry."

"Jeff, I want your support in this. I need your support."

"Why do you need my support? I have known you for like three months," he said. Jeff always trivialized our relationship, narrowing it down to a weekly window, when he was pissed at me. It was like how mothers told their baby's ages in terms of weeks instead of months.

"Actually nine. We could have had a baby in that amount of time."

"Thank God that didn't happen."

"Hey! What crawled up your ass?"

"Nice language. That's hot."

"No, seriously. What's the matter? I have tried talking to you since that night, and you keep brushing me off, and it's getting really tired."

"I'm not brushing you off," he said. "I don't know. I guess I just didn't think things would end up this way."

"What way?" I asked.

"Just like a mess. Everything was fine till we got all drunk that night."

"It's not a big deal, I thought. You even said that. Can we just put it behind us? Cash it up to another drunk night? You've had plenty of those."

"Thanks. Cheap shot. You know it's different."

I wondered how this happened, that I was actually now the "guy" in the situation.

"I know. I'm sorry. I'm just so confused and scared and…"

"Don't be scared. You're going to be fine. I'm just giving you shit," Jeff said. It was sweet how even when he was pissed, he was trying to take care of me.

"Actually, I have some news too."

"What's that?"

"Jessica and I are engaged."

My stomach did a reverse flip, cannonball style. So much for having the upper hand in this situation. He wasn't upset about me at all, apparently.

"Wait a minute. You are giving me shit, and you're *engaged*?"

"I'll take that as a congratulations?"

"Sorry. Congratulations." A thick silence rolled in like Cape fog. "Well, then I guess we're both happy for each other. Glad we had this lunch to share our wonderful news."

We barely spoke for the remainder of the lunch. I pretended to read *The Enterprise,* and Jeff pretended not to notice the swollen air hovering above. He even whistled at one point after finishing his sandwich. This time, I did mind sitting in silence with Jeff. It was deafening. It was as though there was nothing left to say between us. Our friendship had changed. Maybe we were never friends to begin with, I thought. I guess the old saying is true: guys and girls can't be friends.

∧

Jeff and I didn't communicate for the following week. It was lonely, but it made it easier for me to think about moving and leaving my life in Woods Hole behind me. I started to see my move as almost a summer away at camp, and now I was going back home to New York. It was as though I had never left. I mean, it was only nine months. Maybe my old apartment in Chelsea would even still have a vacancy. I gave notice to Dr. Manning at work, and it went surprisingly well.

"The acting bug bite you again?" Dr. Manning joked.

"Hardly. I'm so done with that. No, I want to keep doing the psychology thing, and I was hoping you'd maybe write me a recommendation letter for grad school still?"

"Of course...though you did bail out on that two year commitment!"

"I know. I'm sorry. Something just came up, and I need to go back."

"No worries. I've had that "something came up" myself before," he said and winked.

I then saw why Dr. Manning was such a popular psychiatrist. He really was empathetic and understood people, particularly young women.

"Thanks. I feel really bad."

"It's fine, Emma. Really. Let me connect you with some of my folks in New York. Perhaps you can intern, God willing, get a job there while you're applying to school. There are so many great hospitals around Manhattan with psychiatric units."

"That'd be great. Thanks."

I got up to leave and a wave of emotion came over me about Dr. Manning, like he was a brother I never had. I wanted to go in for the hug but thought better of it, as he had already sat down and began checking his messages.

Kimmie and Robin and Claire threw me a going away party during lunch in the unit cafeteria. The Depression and OCD research assistants attended as well, making it look like an actual party. There were Paxil balloons and yellow streamers taped to the walls and a Stop N' Shop sheet cake with white traditional frosting and a rainbow air balloon that had "Bon Voyage!" written on it in green-colored, cursive frosting. The party was bittersweet. I didn't realize I actually cared about any of these people, particularly Kimmie, who called me into her office after she gulped a couple glasses of sangria. "I want to show you something," she said, opening her desk drawer. She pulled out the rock hard, chocolate chip bagel I had left on her desk as a joke to gross her out when I first started the job. "I kept it," she said. "Wow, I'm...flattered?"

"I know you think it's weird, that I'm weird. I am," she said, shaking her head. "But your friendship has meant a lot to me. You took the time to get to know me, and I just really appreciate it...and you, so thanks." She gave me a hug. "I'm going to miss you. Please keep in touch. I know you're always on email, so you have no excuse!" she said. We laughed, knowing that we spent at least a full workday each week just emailing instead of doing data entry.

"No worries. I will," I said.

My mother and Ron arrived over the weekend to help me pack up my apartment. My mother was clutch in these situations. For example, when I left New York, she drove in that morning on the fly, helped me drag all of my stuff down four flights of stairs, and drove me up to Cape Cod, no questions asked. Or, when I thought I was having a heart attack in college, she flew to Chicago to escort me back to New Jersey, knowing full well that I had an anxiety disorder, not cardiac arrest. I knew that my mother thought I was making the right decision when I left New York and ditched acting.

And here she was helping me sort through my clothes, making piles to keep and piles to toss. The toss pile was exponentially larger than the keep, perhaps symbolic of my tossing away this year in Cape Cod and starting anew in New York. Was I moving backwards or forwards, I wondered. When I had packed all of my things, I had only five large trash bags full of clothes (yes, I still had not graduated to *real* luggage in my adult life) and some crappy IKEA furniture--all "toss"-able. It was a sad sight. I guess you could look at is as ascetic, kind of *Into the Wild*-esque, but it was also sort of pathetic and demonstrative of the hobo lifestyle I'd been leading all these years since college. I could literally pack up my entire life and all of my belongings in five hours.

"Well, I think our job here is done," my mother said, sitting on one of my trash bags. It collapsed like quicksand beneath her, and she sunk almost completely to floor-level. She had on her "moving outfit," comprised of brand new, white Keds, spankin' crisp jeans that still had dry cleaning pleats in them (who dry cleans jeans?), and a black and white Wham, t-shirt that read, "Wake Me Up before you Go-Go" that she'd had since the 1980s. The "Go-Go" was written in pink and yellow neon bubble letters.

"Yeah, I guess that was easy," I said, looking around. Dingo was listless, walking back and forth, like a goldfish. He knew something was up, and I could tell he was stressed. His tail was C-shaped, coiling underneath his body, and he didn't eat his breakfast.

"So does Stephen like Dingo?" my mother asked, reaching out to pet Dingo.

"I think so. He never said he didn't like him."

"Well, that's one positive," she said.

"What is that supposed to mean? That there are more negatives?"

"Well, sweetie, you can't expect me not to be concerned. I'm *your mother*." She employed this job title whenever she wanted to excuse a meddlesome or judgmental comment. "I mean, you're not getting any younger, and I just want to make sure you start making adult decisions, put down some roots."

"What do you think I'm trying to do here with Stephen? We are moving in together, mom. This is a big deal."

"I just think this cohabitation stuff these days is garbage," she said, making sure Ron was not within earshot. Ron was outside, rearranging the car trunk. "If a guy wants to make a commitment, then he should propose."

"We are not in the 1950s anymore."

"The same rules apply. I'm just worried you'll end up alone, barren."

"Ugh, do you have to use that word, 'barren?'" I said, looking at her Wham t-shirt, wondering how I was genetically derived from this woman.

"I just don't want life to pass you by."

Once the rotting eggs talk ended, my mother and Ron packed up and left for New Jersey. I looked around the apartment, at the cedar floors covered in dust-bunnies and the few remaining items I had stacked in a corner by the door. It was empty, just the way I found it only nine months earlier. But I was full. I was full of memories of my life in Cape Cod, and I had them to carry me through on my journey back to New York. My time here would make me stronger, I thought…I hoped.

Chapter 10

"Wow, the place looks great," I said, pulling the last trash bag into Stephen's--I mean, "our"--apartment.

"Thanks. I tried. I cleared out half the closet for you in the bedroom, and you can put the rest of your clothes in the hall closet. I moved the card table."

"Really? Your sacred card table?" I thought back to how far we'd come since I sat at that card table for our first rehearsal almost three and a half years ago.

Stephen disappeared into the kitchen and came back carrying a green bottle of Veuve Cliquot champagne and two of those plastic champagne glasses with the removable bottoms.

"To...?" I said, securing the bottom of my glass.

"How about to us--and being mindful of what we have," he said.

"To us and mindfulness," I toasted.

I played along with that whole Buddhism thing. Stephen was a recent convert. I too wanted to learn to be present and listen to my footsteps, but being mindful really interfered too much with the tape running 80 mph in my head.

It was still light outside, and we decided to take our drinks out onto the fire escape out the bedroom window. Stephen had set up an illegal charcoal grill out there, with a patch of green indoor/outdoor grass carpeting, and a chair. It was his attempt at a backyard. We used to love sitting out there on the first warm days of Spring, laughing at all the 20-somethings who immediately busted out their flip flops and shorts, exposing pasty limbs, in the 60-degree weather. The fire escape seemed really small, and, quite honestly, kind of lame compared to my 12-foot long front porch in Cape Cod, equipped with three Adirondack chairs, a Weber electric grill, and a spot for Dingo. Dingo now had his nose pressed up against the screen longingly. But when I looked over at Stephen sitting across from me, with a view of the Hudson River looming far off in the distance, I melted. I wouldn't have traded the vision of him and the Manhattan skyline for any Adirondack chair. I reached across and touched his muscular thigh, giving it a squeeze. He grabbed my hand and put it up to his mouth, kissing it.

"You have no idea how much I've missed you," he said.

"Me too."

We just locked eyes and kept smiling. It was like we were falling in love all over again. I remembered the time after Stephen and I had started working together in acting class, and I asked him to come to see a cover band with me at Fiddlesticks in the West Village after work one night. It was the first time that I asked him to do something "as a friend" and not as a scene partner. I paced back and forth before making the call to invite him, with flutters in my stomach and nervous hands. He emphatically accepted, assuaging any fears I had that he thought of me as strictly-classroom material. And when we heard Pearl Jam "Better Man" play, Stephen and I danced up a storm. He swung me around, and I crashed back hard into his chest, and we couldn't stop laughing and touching each other.

"I can't stop smiling," he said. "My cheeks hurt."

"Me too."

And now on the fire escape it was happening again. My cheeks hurt from smiling so much as we drank the Veuve Cliquot. We reminisced, and I was shocked at how well Stephen remembered everything about our relationship, down to the smallest detail, like how I don't like water chestnuts in my Chinese food and how hand soap, the foamy kind, bothers me--doesn't seem like it gets the job done. (Stephen didn't exactly have the memory of an elephant due to the loads of pot he smoked--I guess he saved some brain cells for certain, enjoyable memories). He climbed through the window to his bedroom and came back out carrying a small scrapbook.

"I made this for you," he said handing it to me.

"How sweet! Oh my God! I remember this," I said, flipping to the first page with a black and white photo of us kissing from a camping trip on Lake George. Stephen had written in silver, paint pen beneath: "Emma and Stephen, 2000-future." "To the future? You have pictures of that too?!"

"Nah. I figured I'd leave those pages blank, and we can fill them in as we go along: wedding pics, baby photos, graduations..." Stephen lit a Parliament Light with his old favorite Zippo that had a Mercedes Benz emblem on the front of it.

I couldn't believe what I was hearing. He had changed so dramatically! Was this for real, I wondered? It was like God had come down and answered my prayers, delivering a new-and-improved Stephen. He said all the right things to keep me from feeling insecure and vulnerable, the only two things I felt in the past with him. As I leafed through the scrapbook pages, we went down memory lane. He had saved everything, from theater tickets and Playbills, which he taped carefully to each black paper page, to menus from restaurants we loved, like Esperanto on Avenue C in the East Village, and matchbook covers from our favorite bars.

"I had no idea you kept all this stuff."

"Well, I had to do something with all that trash around my room you used to complain about." He flicked the cigarette off the fire escape and looked over to make sure no one was on fire.

"And I thought you were just a hoarder. Wow, this is really amazing."

There was the photo from when I had Thanksgiving with Stephen's family, us covered in mud with a football next to his cousins. He included a photo of us performing together that someone from class had taken for the Actor's Studio website.

"I forgot that this was taken," I said. "God, look how thin I was!"

"Stop it. You're just as beautiful as you always were, maybe more so."

The scrapbook ended with a letter that Stephen had written, addressed to me.

"Wait. I never got this. Was is it?"

"It's a letter I never sent. I wrote it after you moved to the Cape. I didn't know where to find you, and I guess I just had some things to get off my chest."

"Can I read it now?"

"That's why I put it in there. But don't read it while I'm sitting here. It's too embarrassing. I bought some appetizers, so I'll go fix them up in the kitchen." Stephen climbed back into his room, and I braced myself for a tough read. It was an apology letter. He mentioned how he knew he had a lot of growing up to do, and he felt like this time by himself had allowed him to do that. He talked about how he realized he took me for granted, and if he had one wish, it'd be that we could be together again, forever. I started to cry, thinking about all the time we'd lost, all the time I'd spent waiting to hear these words that never came. They were here all along, just too far away for me to hear or see. I climbed in to see Stephen. He was chopping onions in the kitchen, listening to the Rolling Stones song *Waiting on a Friend.*

"I love it," I said, falling into him, wrapping my arms around his waist. "And I loved the scrap book too."

"You did?" Stephen threw the onions in the frying pan and they made a loud sizzling noise.

194

"I can't believe you never sent the letter to me."

"I didn't know where to find you. And I don't know, I guess I was scared that you would tear it up or send it back unread." His eyes were tearing up, and I couldn't tell if it was from chopping onions or if he was genuinely emotional.

I felt like we were in *The Notebook,* in the pouring rain on the dock, when she yells to Noah, "Why didn't you ever write?" And they fall back madly in love.

"I probably would have sent it back," I said. He raised his head up off the pillow, throwing my legs off him. "I'm kidding!!! Of course not. If I had only known sooner...I would have been here sooner. Think of all the time we lost."

"No, now is the right time. I wasn't ready before. Now I am. Think of the all the time we have ahead now."

I pictured that graduation he mentioned, us sitting in the audience with a video camera, applauding our brilliant child, who looked exactly like him, a mini-him. I couldn't have been happier.

∧

With a heavy champagne buzz, topped off with a few Sierra Nevadas, Stephen and I thought it would be fun to go shopping for apartment stuff at The Container Store and Bed Bath N' Beyond in Chelsea. We held hands walking down Seventh Avenue. We passed the Actor's Studio where we took classes, and The Men's Wearhouse where I took Stephen to buy his first suit, which he needed for my friend Stephanie's Newport summer wedding.

"Do you still have that suit?" I asked.

"Yeah, I've worn it a few times--"

"I don't want to know," I said, picturing him at a wedding swinging around some trashy whore in a tight red dress with a slit up the side.

"--as a costume!" he continued. "Sensitive little one, aren't we?"

"I'm a Cancer. We're like that." We passed the Taco Bell where I ran into Stephen a few weeks after he dumped me. I was walking past the front windows on my way home from work (I don't eat Taco Bell after my friend Mike told me he once pissed in the meat when a customer infuriated him). I saw Stephen sitting inside with a chimicanga, staring off into space. I knocked on the windows, and we waved awkwardly. I wanted to go in, to hug him and tell him I missed him and hadn't eaten in days, but I stopped myself and just kept going.

"Believe me, Bun," he said, "I know you're sensitive."
My inclination to be "sensitive" has been pervasive
throughout my life, particularly in childhood. I was
desperately afraid of being kidnapped and spent a lot of
time taking measures to prevent it. For example, when I
broke my foot in the fifth grade from falling off a
hammock, I wore the Fred Flintstone-like shoe on my
cast, even when I went to sleep. This, I figured, would
enable me to run if a kidnapper came into my room to
steal me late at night. And I was extremely afraid of
being late--fearing that I'd get "in trouble," two words
that often came out of my mouth. I was so terrified of
being late to school that I had my father drop me off on
his way to work at the hospital, at 7 a.m. I turned the
lights on in the school hallways each morning, as I beat
everyone to the punch. School didn't begin until 8:30,
so I would be sort of the welcoming committee and
knew all the janitors, the first to arrive, quite well. I also
had a sensitive stomach and was known to carry at least
three types of antacids with me at all times. They came
in particularly handy before I had a show, and I drank
liquid Pepto like it was water. I truly was not suited for
the performing arts with nerves like mine.

Stephen grabbed a Smurf-blue colored plastic cart at Bed Bath N' Beyond and started down past the fans on his left into the kitchenware section. He started browsing the mini sandwich grills and fell in love with "The Samm'ich Master."

"So awesome," he said, lifting the box up to eye level.

"So college...really?" I asked.

"Nothin' like late-night cheesy melts."

"I thought you quit smoking weed," I said.

"I did. Just love a good melt, that's all. No need to get hostile on The Master. Give it some love."

I kissed the outside of the box and tossed it in the cart. We passed the backyard/outdoor tools and gadgets area, which was teensy compared to the one in Wal-Mart in the Falmouth Mall--fire escapes don't have much lawn maintenance. Then we headed down the escalator to bedding. I ran and leapt onto the Lilly Pulitzer, flowered display bed.

"Can we get some of these shams and a bed skirt?" I asked?

"The only skirt I want in my room is the one on the floor that I rip off of you." He jumped on top of me and we started kissing. I closed my eyes, but could still feel the hot, white overhead lights shining down on us.

"We should get up before someone tells us to get a room," I laughed.

"Oh, okay…It was just getting good," he said.

"Um really? So not going to third base on the display bed in Bed Bath N' Beyond."

"It'd be a good story to tell the kids," he said.

I convinced Stephen to get a bed skirt and some shams, as long as they were navy in color. They were "man skirts" that way. We bought several of those useless pillows that are used solely for decoration during the day and lay on the floor at night. And we got a nightstand for my side of the bed. It was all coming together, the apartment…and us.

Chapter 11

When I woke the next morning at 8 a.m., Stephen was still fast asleep. The bedroom was pitch black, thanks to the thick, velvet, black stage curtains that hung from the windows. They blocked out any and all light, catering to Stephen's vampire lifestyle. I got up and saw that Dingo was by the kitchen door, waiting to go out. We walked down Eighth Avenue to the nearest newsstand, and I picked up a copy of *Backstage*, the weekly newspaper for performers. *Backstage* is the go-to for casting calls if you don't yet have an agent. It lists union and non-union auditions, as well as ads for directors seeking mail-in submissions of headshots and resumes. Almost everyone in New York who starts out as an actor, singer or dancer purchases *Backstage* weekly and holds onto it like the Holy Grail. I remembered working at Village restaurant and flipping through the pages of *Backstage* with all the other actor/waiters as we ate our "family meal" before our shift. It always depressed me that each and every one of us, in just this one tiny restaurant, had submitted our headshots to the same casting notice. It conjured up images of a thick bottleneck, traffic jam, with so many actors and so few jobs.

"I bought you a copy of *Backstage*," I said, pouring Stephen a cup of coffee when he emerged from bed at noon.

"Cool, thanks. Good to see you," he said and kissed me on the cheek.

"Good to see you too."

"Wow, I can't believe you are really here now."

"I know. Kinda crazy, right? But it feels different this time," I said.

"Yes, it does. Come here," he said, pulling me next to him on the couch. He smelled like sleep. "I missed you when I was sleeping. I was afraid you'd be gone when I woke up."

"No, I'm not going anywhere," I said.

"Good."

Stephen and I went back to bed and laid there till around 3:45 p.m., before his dinner shift at Spollini's. I forgot what it was like living on the restaurant schedule and was nervous about filling my time at night while alone. My friend Kara still lived in the city, but almost all the others had taken the domestic train and moved out to Connecticut or Cobble Hill, Brooklyn and were having babies at an alarming rate. When Stephen left for work, I decided to do some innocent snooping. He always carried around a set of index cards and a pencil, to make note of things that struck him as interesting that he could employ later into his acting. The cards were often strewn about his room, but the bulk of them were in his top desk drawer, I remembered, and I wanted to check them out. Sometimes the notes were completely innocuous, such as, "Man and woman eating breakfast, reading paper, not speaking." Other times, they were potentially loaded, such as "Hot girl in green stilettos-- dark feelings." Whenever I found one of these more loaded cards before, it would send me into a tailspin, wondering just who this hot girl was and what exactly he meant by "dark" feelings. I'd try to casually slip it into our conversations, like "Do you ever get dark feelings?" but he was always onto me and started hiding his cards better or taking them with him in his backpack to work.

I opened his top drawer and found an old pack of Parliament Lights, a red Swiss Army knife, a copy of David Mamet's *Glen Gary, Glen Ross*, a Verizon bill, and, alas, several index cards. Scribbled in his half-cursive, half print style was: "Homeless man--Jesus?", "Father reading book: *Teenage Angst*," and "Emma's lips." Huh, I always thought they were one of my best features. I was glad he noticed too…and relieved not to find anything potentially disconcerting on the cards. My cell phone rang, and it was Jeff.

"Hey there!" I said emphatically picking up. I hadn't spoken to Jeff in a couple weeks after our awkward talk in the sandwich shop. It felt like forever.

"Hey. I just wanted to call to say hi and see how the move went," he said. He sounded uncomfortable.

"Thanks. It went well. Yeah, things are good," I said, shuffling Stephen's index cards.

"Good."

Silence.

"So, wait, how are things going with Jessica? Picking out colors and destinations for the big day?" I asked.

"Something like that…No, I just drove by your house on the way home. It looks empty. It made me really sad."

A rush of emotions flooded me. I missed Woods Hole and wanted desperately to be sitting on my front porch with Jeff having a 5:05 p.m. cocktail.

"Wait, now I'm sad too. So no one has moved in?"

"No, I don't think so. I think I might just go and have a beer on your porch anyway. Maybe it'll become like my clubhouse. Jessica moved in now, so I need somewhere to go while she watches *Five Minute Meals with Rachel Ray*."

"Sounds blissfully domestic."

I pictured Jessica in a pink apron with hearts on it whipping up some vegan-delight for dinner.

"Well, that's all I got, really," he said. "Just wanted to check in."

"No, thanks...I missed talking. I *miss* talking. So we're still friends?"

"Yeah, something like that," he said.

When Jeff and I hung up, I felt a pang of nostalgia for the good old days, just the two of us. I remembered our first conversation about Stouffers pizza at The Food Buoy and the time he drove all the way to Maine to find a Friendly's that had a Jubilee Roll for my birthday cake (they're my fave). I wondered if we'd actually remain friends years from now, when he was married to Jessica and I was, well, who knows with Stephen. Marriage was not Stephen's favorite subject. He hedged every time I brought it up in the past, referencing his father's late nuptials at the age of 46 (to a woman 10 years his junior, P.S.)-- as if this was some kind of solace, to know that his father finally took the plunge when he was getting regular colonoscopies and had lost some all of his hair.

Stephen came home from work around 11:30 that night. I had tea light scented soy candles lit and scattered about the apartment, and I set out a bottle of Cabernet. The Amos Lee song *Trouble* was playing when he arrived.

"Party for one?" he said.

"Well, now it's for two." I gave him a hug. He was still sweaty from work and smelled like brick oven pizza smoke.

"I have to shower," he said.

"You okay?" His lack of enthusiasm was jarring.

"Yeah. I just need to regroup when I come home from work. I've been smiling and talking for the past three fucking hours." He sharply tossed his backpack onto the kitchen floor and headed to the bathroom.

"Did something bad happen?"

"No, Emma. Nothing *bad* happened, per se…other than my fucking job. I just can't really deal with waiting tables anymore. I mean, this is not what I pictured myself doing. I am an actor, not a fucking waiter."

"I know that. We both know that. But you are just making money so that you can be an actor. Only, what, like 2 percent of people make their living solely as an actor."

"Where'd you learn that, in your "Intro to Theatre" class at Northwestern?"

Stephen hated the fact that I went to a private college. He thought it was "wasteful" when I could have gone to a state school, like he did.

"Wait a minute, I'm just trying to help here."

"I know. Sorry. Really. I just…like I said, sometimes I just need to regroup after work, and be alone."

The "alone" word again. The last time I heard it was during the Honey Bunches of Oats talk. I felt the urge to kick him, hard.

"Noted," I said and grabbed my coat.

"Wait, where are you going? You don't have to leave…"

"It's fine, really." My face was hot and my throat was closing up. "Come on, Dingo. Let's go for a walk."

Dingo shot up off the couch and followed me out the door. As we walked down Eighth Avenue, I was fuming and petrified at the same time. What had I done? Was this a mistake? I could be having beers at the The Captain Kidd with Jeff and Ricky Coldcuts, and here I was, alone, window shopping in the middle of the night, feeling too uncomfortable to go back to my own apartment. The fact was, it was still his apartment, and no matter how much stuff I had there, it would always be his. I grabbed a *New York Times* and sat on a park bench in front of Empire Diner on 29th and 10th. I looked down at my cell phone to see if I had missed a call from Stephen. I hadn't.

Two hours later, I came home and found Stephen still awake, drinking a glass of Cabernet on the couch. His face had change; it was softer.

"I'm sorry," he said. "I didn't mean to be a complete asshole."

"Well, you were."

"I know. Please forgive me. This is not how I want this to go."

I wondered what he meant by that, as if he had some greater idea of where it was going.

"How do you want it to go? Because I'm feeling confused and not too comfortable." He reached for my hand and pulled me next to him. I leaned in and found it hard to stay angry.

"I'm sorry, Bunny. Really." Stephen always called me Bunny when he was sorry.

"Well just don't do it again…that "alone" crap. You know how I feel about it."

"Noted," he said, poking me in the ribs. I couldn't help laughing.

Though Stephen was not exactly funny, per se, in the technical sense of the word, he did crack me up. We created characters together, like "Harold and Hannah Bickerson," who bickered all the time but always make up and dashed off to their splendid, sprawling home in East Hampton. The Bickersons, we decided, had protruding underbites and spokes with an affectation of "the rich" and with large hand gestures. They loved to talk about high-society New York, like the charity balls and Fashion Week, something which neither Stephen nor I knew much about being struggling actors. Another character Stephen did was that of The Baby. He spoke in this silly baby voice and would break down and fall on the floor in spasms when he didn't get his way--like in the third aisle of a Duane Reade. And we'd joke about him drinking out of sippy cups because he always spilled, and his needing diapers because he always had to pee. I loved when he'd play The Baby, because then I could take care of him, my most favorite thing to do. I liked when he relied on me and was vulnerable, like when he was sick with a 110-degree fever, and I stayed in bed nursing him with a cold washcloth on his forehead, despite the fact that I hate germs and would have gone running if it had been anyone else. I didn't care. I wanted his germs. Then there was the time that he went into a depression and simply could not bring himself to go to work or class for days. I too the skipped work and class, sitting by his side like Florence Nightingale just to reassure him and make sure he was all right. Stephen did his best to lighten the mood when I got home from walking around that night, even folding a cloth napkin from his kitchen and wearing it as an ascot to play Harold Bickerson. I knew he was trying, so I chose to let go of the hurt and focus on the present. Huh, maybe I was becoming more mindful.

∧

I decided to follow up on some job leads that Dr. Manning had given me in New York. I was supposed to meet with a psychiatrist at New York State Psychiatric Institute, and she worked on the Schizophrenia Unit. Schizophrenia was always a huge scare of mine. My friend Becka's mom got when we were in middle school, and she tried to kill herself with carbon monoxide poisoning while sitting in the garage. She was 35-years-old, same as me. How could someone go from being completely normal, functioning, with a family and job one day to schizophrenic the next, I wondered? I never understood that. Neither did Becka's family. But I had about a year to go until I was in the clear. Apparently, women after 35 rarely, if ever, get schizophrenia.

Riding the A train up to 168th Street for the interview, a man with red hair sat across me. He was reading *The Atlantic* and looked like an academic. Maybe he worked at Columbia Teachers' College, I thought. He looked up at me and smiled, and in that instant, I thought of Jeff and missed him terribly. I grabbed my cell phone out, ready to send a text, but was on the train and unable to distract myself and get that instant gratification of communicating in cyberspace. Instead, I had to be alone with my thoughts, which at this moment revolved around the potentially grave mistake I'd made in handling things the way that I did after Jeff and I hooked up. I was such an idiot, I thought! He was being normal about the whole thing, concerned for my stupid feelings, and all I could do was shit on him, the perhaps only real friend I had on the Cape, while focusing on Stephen, the man who shat on me! I wanted to get away from myself and my own selfish-baby thoughts, so I struck up a conversation the red headed academic sitting across from me on the train.

"So, do you work at Teacher's College?" I asked.

"Excuse me?" he said, looking up from the journal.

"Sorry...I didn't mean to bother you." I lied.

"No, um, yeah...I do work there. Wait, how'd you know?" he asked, searching for clues that had given him away. He adjusted his brown, tortoise shell glasses.

"I don't know. It's a talent of mine, compartmentalizing people based on their looks," I said.

He laughed. "Well, that's quite the 'talent.' I am sure you could put that to good use, a real resume builder."

"I know. I should put it under "Special Skills." God, I wish I could, like make a job of it. I'm really good at compartmentalizing just about everything: people, feelings, mistakes..." Wait, hello!? Why was I dumping all of my issues on this innocent MTA passenger? As if the stench of hot Miller Lite that coated the sticky floor of the subway wasn't bad enough, I had to be *that* girl.

"'Well, I guess it's better than rumination," he said. "At least you can put it away and move past it."

"Good point. I bet you'll make a great teacher."

"Thanks."

I watched out the train windows as we moved above ground from 116th Street, passing tall red brick buildings and the Columbia Theological Seminary on our way to the 125th Street stop. The nameless redheaded man shot up from his seat.

"Well, good luck with everything," he said.

"Yeah, you too."

He walked off and looked back at me as the train pulled out of the station. Part of me felt an urge to jump off the train in that moment, run up to him, and tell him that I thought I was in love with him, kind of like in the Gwyneth Paltrow movie *Sliding Doors*. But then I wondered, was it him, or was it the red hair that made me think of Jeff, and maybe I was in love with Jeff? Or was I still in love with Stephen? Of course I was in love with Stephen, I told myself. Wasn't I?

∧

Chapter 12

The New York State Psychiatric Institute was looming and large. It had recently been renovated with huge panels of green glass on the exterior. It resembled a terrarium or a large Pellegrino bottle. I walked in the front, and the security guard called up to Dr. Lilly, whom I was meeting on the Schizophrenia Unit. He called the elevator for me, which had an elevator operator, who had to unlock each floor with a key. There was tight security in this place, unlike at the Eating Disorder's Unit back in Cape Cod. When the elevator opened onto the unit, I faced a large semicircle reception desk, with two nurse behind it. I expected her to be Nurse Rathchett from One Flew Over the Cookoo's Nest, but it was a 50-something woman with grey hair, large red-framed glasses, a la Sally Jesse Rafael, and clad in butterfly scrubs.

"You have an appointment?" she asked curtly.

"Yes. I'm here to see Dr. Lilly?"

"One moment."

She called Dr. Lilly on the phone and told me to have a seat in the waiting room. The Unit was scary. I could hear screaming coming from what was called "The quiet room," where patients who were having a psychotic break got a time out. It was what you'd imagine "the loony bin" felt like. Some patients were walking down the hall, mesmerized, mouths agape and lacking any affect, typical of a person with schizophrenia. The walls were eggshell white and the chairs were maroon plastic leather with hard springs that you felt sitting on the cushion.

"Hello, Emma?" Dr. Lilly said, extending her hand.

"Yes," I replied, standing and trying to appear perky even though I was frightened and wanted to go home.

"Let's head back to my office so we can talk in private."

We passed several rooms along the way. One was a recreation or game room, where patients sat. Some were staring out the window or at the television, and others were reading or playing cards. Most of the patients were men, in what seemed to be their 30s or 40s, and there was one woman with unkempt, frizzy black hair, who was cradling a baby doll made out of nylons. In the next room we passed was a meeting room, where patients sat in a circle around a therapist. I assumed it was some type of group therapy. And then we passed a few of the patient's private rooms, all very somber with nothing but a twin metal bed with maroon-colored, coarse blankets, the kind you'd use for a horse. The screaming continued in The Quiet Room in the background but faded out as we approached Dr. Lilly's office.

"Sorry 'bout that," she said, smiling. "That doesn't freak you out, does it?"

"No, not at all," I lied. "I'm used to it. My dad's nuts." Wait, seriously!? Did I just freaking say that? I wanted to crawl under one of the horse blankets and hide.

"Huh," she sad. I could tell this interview was going South rapidly. "So tell me what you're looking to do here and a little bit about what you did with Dr. Manning in the Eating Disorders Unit."

"Well, I'm interested in going back to school for my Ph.D. in clinical psychology, and I thought I'd like to get some more research experience and work with a different subset of patients."

"Well this experience and these patients will surely be different," she said, taking copious notes with a Risperidol pen. "Did you like working with Dr. Manning?"

"I loved it," I said. I pictured the long therapy-centric lunches Kimmie, Robin, Claire and I had sitting in a semicircle on the sea foam green carpet. Or when we'd play "Guess the Disorder," taking turns giving each other clues of symptoms the patient experienced from the DSM-IV Diagnostic Manual and we'd have to guess what they suffered from. "Bipolar!" we'd yell.

"Well here on the schizophrenia unit, things are a bit different because the patients are inpatient, not outpatient, so you will have more clinical interaction than you did in the eating disorders unit. Will be that okay with you?"

I knew that I must reply affirmatively, so I did.

"I'll have you do things like ask the patients what's the date, who the President is, where they are, et cetera, to assess where they are with the symptomatology each day. Most patients on medication will be lucid and know the answers to these questions, but others who may be having a psychotic episode or break may not."

"Right," I said. "I'm fine with that. Sounds really interesting." I was scared to death. Psychotic break? What if they grew angry and decided to take it out on me, stabbing me with a Resperidol pen?

"Terrific. Well let me go over some other things with you, and we can talk about a schedule and when you can get started. Sound good?"

"Perfect."

Dr. Lilly showed me around the rest of the unit, where I'd sit, and she introduced me to another research assistant named Alice. Alice wore small, gold-rimmed glasses, like those of an accountant, and she had sandy blonde, shoulder length hair. She was a bit overweight and she smelled like seaweed.

"Nice to meet you," Alice said. "So you're the newbie?"

I hadn't heard the word "newbie" since I rushed Kappa Alpha Theta at Northwestern. Was Alice a sorority girl? She didn't seem the type.

"Guess so," I said smiling. "Nice to meet you too."

Dr. Lilly and I figured out a schedule that would work for both of us, and she said she'd give me a call after giving me some time to think it over. I had already thought it over, imagining myself sitting next to Alice, smelling seaweed (which reminded me of the Cape, so it wasn't so bad), and looking out the bleak Pellegrino-green windows. There was no carpet to sit on at lunch, just hard brown tile, and the choice of the Columbia Presbyterian Hospital cafeteria or the muffin and bagel cart on the corner of 168th and Broadway as a food option was less than appealing. I had my answer, which was an emphatic "not interested," but I thought I'd let it sink in on the subway ride home before ending all ties with Dr. Lilly.

When I arrived home, Stephen was waiting for me. He had gotten the night off from work at Spollini's and wanted to treat me to a dinner out at Gramercy Tavern. I knew this was way above and beyond affordable for him, but I didn't want to emasculate him. I was flattered that he was trying so hard, but I couldn't shake that regretful voice in my head about Jeff. When Stephen went to take a shower, I decided to call Jeff. Dialing, I paced around Stephen's room, stepping on dirty t-shirts and picked up the dead cactus that had tipped over in his window. Who forgets to water a cactus so much that it dies, I wondered. That is extreme gross negligence, almost intentional and pathological.

"Hey," Jeff said, picking up on the second ring.

"Hey! How are you?"

"Good, yeah…good. You?"

"Good."

"Good."

Silence.

"Well I just wanted to call, because I don't know, I felt like I left and things were kind of bad, and I wanted to say sorry. I think I was just freaking out, and being all stressed and catlike, and--"

"It's fine. I thought things were fine last time we talked. No?"

"Yeah, they were…they are…I don't know. I'm probably just overanalyzing. I think I'm freaking out."

"Really? You? Freaking out? Huh."

I laughed, but the lump in my throat prevented it from being wholehearted. I missed being able to be my complete self with Jeff. He loved me no matter what. With Stephen, I had to pretend that I was someone else--someone casual and completely carefree--the opposite of what I actually was.

"So does town miss me?" I asked, looking for reassurance.

"Well, Ricky Coldcuts misses you. And Scuba Dave is single again on the prowl, so I'm sure he might miss you too."

It was hard to hear about all the characters that seemingly meant nothing to me before, and now I would kill to run into them at the bar.

"And what about you?"

"I don't miss you," he said.

"I wasn't asking that, brat! I was asking how you are!"

"Oh. I'm just kidding…Wow, you are super-sensitive these days. Everything okay in New York?" He purposefully didn't mention Stephen, and I felt bad mentioning him too.

"Um, it's okay. Not bad, not great. Ya' know." I stepped on Stephen's sticker-covered skateboard that was lying out on the middle of the room and started rocking back and forth on it.

"Yeah. Well, you can always come back here," he said.

"Can I? I'd feel like a complete loser, like I failed here, again, and came running back."

"You're not a loser if you come back here, Emma.

Thanks a lot! That doesn't say much about us locals."

"Oh you're a *local* now?" I scoffed, as Jeff and I hated how the "locals" on the Cape prided themselves on their residential status and loathed all outsiders. Locals even wore flip flops that had a white decal reading "Locals" on the strap. I don't think you needed to provide an electric bill or piece of mail to buy a pair though. I'd definitely spotted some summer folks sporting them on the sly.

"So how's Jessica?"

"Good."

"Is she turning into a *Bridezilla* yet, planning her vegan wedding? Wait, are you going to have like a gross vegan cake too?" I got off the skateboard and lay down on the bed, kicking my feet up onto the side of the wall. It was cold on my hot feet.

"Yep, and a "green" theme to boot. Our colors are grass and sage green."

"You did not just say that…what has she done to you? You're like neutered and metro sexual now, referencing colors only found in the J Crew palette. Wait, so with this green motif, I don't even get a paper invitation? Tell me you're not sending an E-vite to your wedding. Your mom will die."

"No, my mom nixed that one. No, you know, just like more eco-friendly, like no gas-guzzling shuttle buses, locally grown food--"

"Hemp linens and a bamboo dance floor? I can just see all the Minolos and Laboutin stilettos getting stuck in those reeds. Actually, on second thought, it's the Cape. Most people will be in clogs."

"Well aren't you Miss Manhattan? Listen, Snotty McSnot, maybe you can scale back and wear flats that day. Actually, I think Jessica is planning to have a basket of flip flops for all the ladies to change into at the front of the tent."

I wanted to barf. I struggled listening to Jeff talk about a basket of flip flops "for the ladies." He sounded like he was on *The Bachelor* talking to Host Chris Harrison about all the "lovely ladies" he had to choose from. Disconcerting, to say the least.

"Well, sounds like Jessica has it all figured out. So things with you two are good?"

"Yeah, great."

"Good. I'm happy for you." I said, picking the chipped candy red nail polish off my toes.

"No you're not. You hate her."

I laughed. I did hate her. Well, "hate" might be too strong of a word...Actually, no, screw it; it was spot on. I hated her.

"I gotta run," Jeff said. "We're going to dinner at Landfall tonight with her parents to talk about more wedding stuff."

"Have a Forbidden Martini for me." The Forbidden Martini was my absolute fave drink at The Landfall-- fresh pomegranate and lime juice, Cointreau, and Grey Goose vodka over shaved ice.

"Okay. Hope things get better there for you."

"Thanks...I miss you."

"Yeah, okay. Talk to you later," he said.

No "I miss you" in return.

Stephen came into the room with a towel around his waist, smelling of Pert and freshly shaven. I felt supremely guilty, as if I had cheated on him. I was secretive and that bothered me. I didn't want that kind of relationship. I wanted to be open with everything, all of my thoughts and feelings, pour them out onto the table and have him accept them and love them no matter what. Then, I went back to reality.

"You okay?" he asked. "You look sad."

"Yeah, fine." I envisioned an older version of myself screaming in The Quiet Room with no one visiting and no family to speak of.

"Well don't take the job then, Bun."

"I don't think I will."

I wasn't sure if I wasn't going to take the job because it was depressing, or because I wanted to leave New York. Stephen did look sexy in his towel though. His black hair was dripping water droplets onto the floor, as he bent over to put his pink pinstriped boxer shorts on. I had gotten him a pair when I went to Lilly Pulitzer in Nantucket, and he originally ridiculed them but then proceeded to wear them like three times a week.

We both got dressed up for dinner. Stephen wore his gray Banana Republic pants that we bought together for my father's honorary dinner three years' prior and a lavender oxford shirt. I wore a BCBG black skirt and a ruby red ruffled, silk tank top with heels. It felt nice to be dressed up together and going on an official date. I decided to make the most of it and to stop spiraling about Jeff. I no longer wanted to think about if I was making the right life decisions. I wanted to just "be." I longed for my early-20s when making decisions really was no big deal: if you made a wrong choice, you just put it behind you and did something else; you had plenty of time ahead. But being in my 30s, these years were more precious, and the mistakes you made, be it about career or relationships, were part of your record, like they were written in permanent ink. I hated that.

Dinner at Gramercy Tavern was delish. I had the pork loin and Stephen ordered the scallops. We shared a nice bottle of Kim Crawford Riesling and stopped by Vesuvio's for an old-school Italian cannoli on our way home. New York was amazing at night, the way it was still bustling even at 11 p.m. In Woods Hole, it was tumbleweeds rolling down the street the moment the sun went down. The only sounds were the squeaking of the metal signs swinging back and forth in the winter wind above the Shucker's Raw Bar alley. The only people to be found were in The Leeside drinking some beers, and even they went home by 9:30. And forget about getting a late-night bite to eat. You were shit out of luck if you forgot to order by 8:30. The only option then was to drive to 7-11 in Falmouth and microwave a hot pocket. New York, on the other hand, you couldn't tell the difference between 8 p.m. and 2 a.m. on a Saturday night in most neighborhoods.

^

The next day, I went down to the West Village to meet my friend Kara for coffee at Doma on the corner of 7th Avenue and Charles Street. Doma was somewhat of a celeb coffee shop, though totally low-key and extremely small. When I walked up to the coffee bar to order, I heard a familiar voice behind me--it was Kerri Russell from the late-90s TV show *Felicity*. She was even more beautiful in person. She looked like a porcelain doll. I wanted to tell her how I thought she messed up choosing Ben over Noel, but thought she may not appreciate the humor, and, yes, it was only a TV show.

"Hey!" Kara said, touching me on the shoulder from behind.

"Hey! I love your new hair!" I said. Kara's former chocolate brown bob was now highlighted with platinum blonde streaks and grown out.

"Thanks. I figured I'd try to go a little more WASPY and blonde, ever since we bagged J-Date. The dark brown hair didn't reel 'em in. They saw right through my and my inability to share feelings and talk about anything personal!" We laughed.

Back in my NYC days, right about when I was hitting rock bottom, Kara and I went on J-Date, the online dating site for Jewish singles, despite the fact that we were both Christian. I had heard it was a better site to meet men, that they were more serious about settling down on that site, as opposed to Match.com or E-Harmony. These women were looking for mothers and life partners, not a quick piece of ass after a couple martinis at The Evelyn Lounge. It was a futile attempt at meeting someone, since we received more hostility than love. Each day, I got at least one email calling me a "shikza," and numerous questions as to why I'd want to date someone of the Jewish faith.

"So would you convert?" a man by the online avatar of "Bored Lawyer" inquired.

"Sure," I typed back, not even thinking twice.

"So what's your deal? Like Jewish meat?" another asked.

"Nah, not a big fan of brisket," I replied.

Bored Lawyer and I emailed back and forth for several weeks but never actually made a date--typical non-committal, New York City guy in his late-20s (but who's bitter?!). I think his mother probably put the kibosh on our impending cyberspace nuptials (yes, I do consider his asking me if I'd convert a cyber proposal). He eventually stopped writing me, and I saw that he continued to update his profile and presumably chat with other girls, those of his own faith. Guess he was bored not only with being a lawyer, but also with emailing me.

Kara and I ordered two Chai tea lattes and cranberry scones and grabbed a seat at the front window table, perfect for watching Felicity, I mean…Kerri Russell. "Wait, where are you coming from? You're all gussied up!" I said.

"Right?" Kara smiled, adjusting the spaghetti straps on her Chanel black tank dress. It occurred to me that her dress was not exactly appropriate for a coffee date during the day. It was more of an evening ensemble. "Wait a minute…are you just coming *home*, you hussy?" I asking taking a huge bite out of my scone. The crumbs stuck to my Mac lip gloss. Kara starting laughing.

"No comment," she replied beaming. "It was really good though!" she said. "I think this one could be a real possibility."

Kara stopped referring to her dates as 'the one" when "the one" turned into about 220 different guys. She was a serial dater, but they were always "one and done," as we said: one date, and a full blackout ensued--she never heard from them again. This, I told her, may have something to do with the fact that she always slept with them on the first date. And, as I already mentioned about Match.com, the men in NYC are out for tail, and if they get it the first night, the chase is over and they move on.

"Did you sleep with him?" I asked, overtly grimacing, fearing the worst.

"Well, not really…sort of."

"What's the 'sort of' part?"

"He didn't get all the way in. I made him pull out, so it only counts as half." She slurped her tea.

"Kara!" I screamed and looked up to see Felicity staring right at me. Shit, this would definitely discourage her from being my new BFF. I am sure she didn't like friends who made scenes in public and drew attention to her.

"*But*," Kara continued, "If you would let me finish, I explained to him that I never do that, so I don't think it was that bad."

"But you *do* always do that."

"No, I don't!" she said defensively. Her face flushed, and I knew I had to drop it. Kara did, in fact, always do this, and she always told the guy afterwards that "she never does this." Nothing had changed since I'd moved. It actually felt strange to be back with Kara at Doma but also completely normal. It was almost as if no time had passed since I had moved to the Cape and now was back. But so much had indeed transpired in that time. I was a new person in an old life. I started to spiral and felt light-headed after a couple sips of Chai.

"I think I might have a panic attack," I said. Kara and I were both prone to anxiety, so talking about panic attacks and various anxiolytic medications was par for the course. "What's up? Are things with Stephen not going well?"

"No, it's not that. Actually, it's quite the opposite. I almost feel like I'm in a *Lifetime* movie titled *A Changed Man*. He really is different now."

"Really? That's great though, no?"

"No, yeah. It's good," I said, picking the cranberries out of my scone. I thought of Kimmie removing the sesame seeds from her bagel and remembered that I owed her a call. "I don't know. It just feels surreal, like something you sort of dreamed but is now happening, and you're watching it from the outside but not really in it."

Kara knew exactly what I meant, and it was comforting to be back with "my people." She wasn't just nodding and pathologizing my behavior. She understood me on a deeper level.

"But it's good though, right? Like, you're happy you moved back?" Kara looked over at Felicity, who was now on her Blackberry. I wondered if Scott Speedman was on the other end of the line.

"Don't be so obvious!" I scolded. "We don't want her to move!"

"Right, no, sorry," Kara said, adjusting her chair to face away from Felicity.

"I think I just need to get a job and figure out what I'm going to do with my life now that I'm like 40."

"You are so not 40! Don't drag me down that path with you! We're 35, which can be closer to 30 than 40 depending on your frame of mind."

"My glass is half-empty. You know that."

"Well fill 'er up. It's depressing. I, for one, am glad you're back. No one freaking goes out around here anymore! All our friends are married and shutting it down. And if I get one more "Happy News!" email announcing a baby or engagement, I might go postal."

"No shit. And the sonograms that people post on Facebook? Could that be more thoughtless? What about all of us women with serious fears of being spinsters or miscarrying?"

I thought of my mother sitting in her "Frankie Says Relax" t-shirt warning me of my impending infertility and thought about ordering another coffee.

"Don't even talk to me about Facebook. I'm so over it," Kara said, checking her phone to see if she got a text message. "After spending the last week stalking my ex, Sam, and then stalking his new girlfriend, I think I need an intervention or just an immediate deactivation."

"So just deactivate."

"I can't. I'll be lonely. It's one of my few remaining social outlets." She continued to check her phone. "Wait, he hasn't texted me to see if I got home okay. Do you think it's over? Was it bad I slept with him?"

I didn't know what to say---what she wanted to hear or the truth, so what I went with the former.

"No, it's fine. Plus, you only half slept with him, and you never do that!" We busted out laughing.

"You bitch. Not everyone can be as perfect as you, Muffy," she scoffed.

"Well don't put all your eggs in this basket. Date lots of people and don't fixate on one. Jeff always told me that guys can smell the desperation from a mile away. And they can also smell other guys on their turf, which of course makes them like the chase more."

"Oh, well, if Yoda Jeff, the dating savant, said it's so, I guess that's true. What's up with you two anyway?"

"What do you mean?"

"I mean, didn't you guys like…" she raised an eyebrow.

"Yes, we did. But we just sort of ignored it and everything went back to normal. And now I'm with Stephen, so."

"Did you ignore it, or did he?"

"We both did."

"I don't know, Emma. I think he's into you."

"He's engaged, Kara, to someone else."

"Whatever. She's his beard to mask how he really feels about you. Let me guess: did the proposal to Jessica come before or *after* you told him you were moving to New York to be with Stephen?" I didn't answer.

"That's what I thought," she said, grabbing her Chai and slurping down the remainder.

"Okay, Nancy Drew. Let's move onto other topics." I actually really wanted to discuss Jeff, but I didn't want to let on to Kara that I was not certain about things with Stephen. I mean, what if Stephen and I got engaged, and Kara was standing at the alter with me, doubting my feelings for him. I couldn't do that to Stephen. But was Jessica maybe Jeff's beard?

"So, wait, should I text him to tell him I got home and had a nice night? He did pay for the drinks, so maybe I owe him a thank you. It's only polite."

"You're reaching. It wasn't dinner; it was drinks. I'd wait on that. Give him a day to get back to you. Remember, he likes the chase."

"Right, right," she said, gulping her Chai Latte, trying to absorb the dating advice that she never truly absorbed. "The chase…"

As I walked home from Doma, trying to get my grass roots exercise (I was too poor to join the gym, and, well, you can't run in NYC), my phone rang. It was Jessica. Now the only reason I had her number as one of my contacts was in case I needed to find Jeff. She had called me one day back in May when she and Jeff were in a fight, seeking my advice. It was a totally awkward conversation, trying to pretend to that we were friends, but I tried to help her out, and since then retained her phone number.

"Hey, it's Jessica!" she squealed.

"Yeah, hey. How are you?" I asked while rolling my eyes. Incidentally, I was in front of The Pleasure Chest on Seventh Avenue, an 'intimacy store' (okay, a sex shop) when she called.

"Goooooooood….gooooooood," she said. Did I mention I hated her?

"What's up?" I wanted to cut to the chase and end this call pronto. I needed to check out some of the new rabbit vibrators and kinky sex toys to spice things up in the bedroom with Stephen. He had told me in the past that I was too cautious, and I wanted to just show him how the Cape had let the dangerous and dirty tigress out in me (um, not really…but the toys might help? Maybe a tigress costume?).

"Well, as you know, Jeff and I are getting married."

"Yep."

"Well, I know how close you two are, so I wanted to ask…" My heart started racing. Please, God, no…don't do it, I thought. "If you'd be one of my bridesmaids!" she continued.

"Wow! Jessica, I'm so flattered." I tried to think of an excuse on the fly--my grandma was sick? Another conflict that day? Ugh. I had nothing. "Sure. That's so nice of you to ask." I picked up and sniffed a mint chocolate scented condom.

"Perfect! I am so happy to have you be a part of it, and I know Jeff will be thrilled."

"I bet he will be!" I laughed to myself. This could possibly be Jeff's worst nightmare, me and Jessica, next to each other up at the alter--the past clashing with the future.

"And I think you know about our green theme, right?"

"Yeah, sounds awesome," I said. "Is my dress hemp?" I balked, shuffling through the various sex kitten numbers hanging from the front store rack. I was never a fan of red lace.

"Hah, hah!" she said. "No, but it is green…well, just in color. It's actually sort of a pea green."

Wait a minute here. What happened to sage and willow, or whatever the fuck the J Crew colors were?! Pea green? Was she serious? I couldn't think of anything more heinous, which was most likely her evil intention, attempting to make herself look prettier.

"Huh," I said. "Okay." I held up a pink and purple lace genie costume in front of the mirror, perfect for 'granting wishes!' Too bad my wish to not be on the phone with Jessica wasn't granted.

"I've already found the dress on the Marc Jacobs website, so I'll just send you the link."

Okay, Marc Jacobs? How much was this split pea soup number gonna cost me, I wondered, not to mention the loads of tailoring I'd need since I had no torso and triple-A cups.

"Sounds good," I said.

"Make sure you get it *soon*, because I don't want them to run out."

Yeah, it'll be the first thing on my list, Jess. I'm sure the pea pod is being snatched off the racks like hot cakes.

"Anything else I should do?" I asked wearily. I wondered if she could sense my indifference bordering on irritation.

"Well, since you asked..."

Guess she couldn't sense it. Kill me. Fast.

"I was wondering if you'd help plan the bachelorette party. It's going to be in May up here on the Cape, and you know the bars better than any of my friends from college."

I couldn't tell if this was a dig--like I was the alcoholic lush, who was best friends with her fiancé--or, if she genuinely thought I'd throw a good party, which, let's be honest, is one thing I'm good at. But me throwing her bachelorette party? I mean, the irony in that! The one person who hates her the most is not only in the wedding but now throwing the bach party. Something was fishy here.

"Um, sure, I guess," I said. "But I'm all the way in New York now. I wont really know where to go."

"Nothing ever changes around here. You know that."

"Well, sure," I said. Ironically, I was now in the Bachelorette Party section of The Pleasure Chest, chock full o' plastic penis straws, Hottie whistles, blow up stripper dolls, and penis cake mix.

"Great. I'm sending you an email Excel spreadsheet with my girls' emails and addresses as we speak." I could hear her typing and imagined her French manicured tips tapping away at the keyboard.

Did I mention I hated her?

"Sounds good. Well, listen, I gotta run, but I'll be in touch," I said. "And thanks again for the invite."

"No problemo," she said. "TTYL!"

Ew.

When I got back to the apartment, Stephen was building a small gazebo--no joke--in the living room. He had planks of wood strewn about, extending from the far kitchen wall and almost reaching the bedroom. Lucky for him, the apartment was railroad-style in layout and the length of it accommodated such a project.

"Tell me you're not going to put this on the fire escape," I said. "Are you building a backyard?"

"It's for my acting class. It's an 'activity,'" he said, intensely hammering nails. The sound was jarring, so much so that Dingo was hiding underneath the bed. I could see his two brown and white front paws sticking out from under the box spring.

"What's an activity?" I asked, genuinely interested.

"It's Meisner."

I knew who Sanford Meisner was and his acting technique on a basic level, but this whole "activity" thing was new to me. Apparently, Meisner taught that staying "active" or doing a very difficult and emotional "activity" on stage, such as gluing a meaningful broken vase back together, writing a last testament and will to your children, or, in this case, building a gazebo, would help you be a better actor.

"So what's the meaning behind the gazebo?" I asked.

"It's for a marriage proposal."

My heart skipped a beat. Marriage proposal? To me? Wait, so was this part of acting, or was this for real? And was he then really thinking about proposing, like this was something on his mind, or was this part of the scene? I was confused…but also sort of secretly thrilled. Maybe he would use the gazebo for class and do the proposal as a dress rehearsal before doing the real deal at home for me! Holy shit, I didn't have anything to wear. And what would everyone say when I called them to tell them we got engaged so quickly? What would my mom say? Well, she'd be happy that it would be the end of my "barren" future. My dad? Well, he'd just continue reading the paper without blinking an eye. And Jeff? What would Jeff think?

"Do you mind not stepping on that piece?" Stephen growled. My fantasy came to a screeching halt.

"Oh, sorry." I stepped over the wood and moved into the hallway, shouting over the hammering. "Did you eat?" I asked.

"I'm fine," he said and picked up the piece of wood I had just stepped on. He sanded where my foot had been.

"Well are you hungry, or going to be? I can go get some stuff at the market. Maybe make steaks and 'shrooms or?"

"I just need to finish this, Emma." I knew he was not interested since he used my name in that "you're a child in trouble who did something bad" sort of way. I walked back to our room and sat on the bed. Dingo came out from below and joined me. I didn't know what to do with myself. The TV was in the living room, where Stephen was, so I couldn't watch *Oprah*, (too bad, 'cause it was on letting out your inner sex kitten). And it was too loud to read or concentrate on anything. I felt trapped. I could go back outside, but I had just come from there. That's the problem I found with Manhattan. When you're out on the streets, you start to feel claustrophobic and irritated and want to go indoors. But when you go back home to your apartment, often the size of a dog's crate, you immediately feel claustrophobic there and need to go back out. Out and in, out and in…it's a viscous cycle. I looked over on Stephen's desk and saw that there were several new index cards. No harm I reading them, right? It's not like they were a journal or something, and there they were just sitting out in the open, begging to be read and interpreted…or misinterpreted. I picked them up and flipped through them:

"Heat on Tenth Avenue sidewalk," "Coffee Buzz" and…"Gansevoort shower." Hold on a minute here…Gansevoort Shower? As in The Hotel Gansevoort in the Meat Packing District? What was he doing there? And when did he get a chance to see the shower? More importantly, with *whom*? I knew he could never financially swing a night at The Gansevoort, and if he was planning a surprise overnight with me, he knew I didn't like having sex in the shower. I thought of the time he went down on me in the shower, while I stood above him straddling awkwardly. Stephen started to choke on the waterfall streaming off my body and into his nose, and he promptly fell over the side of the tub in a coughing fit resembling a beached whale with his white ass laying on my roommate's lavender shaggy bathmat. It was embarrassing--for him--to say the least, kind of like a porno remake of *Free Willie.*

The hammering and sanding continued in the living room. I put the cards back on his desk as I'd found them and pondered how to react to the shower index card. Should I say anything? But then he'd know I read them. But I mean, he always knew I read them. What would be so different? But things were going so well. Did I need to ruin them? Maybe it was an innocuous little fantasy! Or maybe it was merely he helped a friend fix the shower at The Gansevoort. Surely one of his acting buddies worked as a plumber or concierge at the hotel on the side, no? An indigestible looming sense of vulnerability cast a pall over me and I need to get out and fast.

"I'm going to grab a coffee and walk the dog," I said walking through the planks of wood like I was playing hopscotch. Dingo was reluctant to go near the mass of wood, so I yanked at his collar, Caesar Milan style, and pulled him unwillingly out the door.

I decided to call Jeff. I needed some comfort. And maybe he'd have some thoughts on the shower card. After all, he was the dating guru and always quick to put out mental fires I'd ignited from nothing. I was like Janet on *Three's Company*, notorious for suffering from a misunderstanding. I hoped this shower inkling would also be a misunderstanding and Jeff could play the role of Jack Tripper enlightening me and assuaging all of my fears.

"So I think Stephen is having an affair," I said to Jeff. I was walking down Ninth Avenue and stopped in front of the Tasti D'Lite. There was a bench out front next to the specials board. Just so happens, Oreo Cookie and

Cheesecake, my fave, were the day's flavors. I took a seat.

"What makes you think that?"

"Well, I found one of his index cards--"

"Oh, God, Emma. I'm not sure I can listen to this," Jeff said. "He is so painful with this affected artist bullshit. He's still making those freaking things?"

"Fine, forget it," I said rifling to see if I had enough change for a small sugar cone.

"No, go on. I'm sorry."

I told Stephen about the shower card and all of the possible best and worst case scenarios.

"So what do you think?"

"I think he cheated on you," Jeff said.

Dingo squatted and took a poop right in front of Tasti D' Lite. It was soft and came out sort of like the soft serve yogurt.

"What!?? Why?" It's amazing how when the voice of reason confirms your worst fears you are in utter shock, as though it can't actually be true.

"Well, I mean, what else could it mean? Doesn't he write these index cards based on some kind of personal experience he has, or are they fantasy-driven?" I was silent, my mind spinning. "Wait, seriously, I can't *believe* I even know this and am talking about it as though it's a *normal* thing to do."

"What should I do?" I asked. I felt sick...so sick that I wasn't able to even get an Oreo and Cheesecake yogurt twist, which was the real tragedy there.

"I don't know. Ask him about it, just straight out. Say, "Who did you fuck in the shower at The Gansevoort?""

"Ew, can you not be so crass?"

"Sorry...who did you *make love to*...is that better?"

"No, that's worse! Do you think he was making love? Like, maybe he's actually in love with someone else?"

"Honestly, you're spiraling out. You need to stop. Get your frozen yogurt, take a deep breath, go for a walk, and then go home and talk to him about it. What do I know? Maybe it's all a big misunderstanding and the card means nothing."

I looked down at Dingo, who was licking the yogurt droppings that fell on the street from a little girl's cone. "Okay. I'm gonna go."

"Are you okay? Do you want me to come get you?" Jeff asked. This was the first time he'd really been nice to me since our fight and the hook up. "I can be there in four hours."

"You'd do that? What about Jessica?"

"Whatever. She'd deal with it. Seriously, you want me to come?"

I actually sort of did. I wanted to see Jeff's freckled face, lean on his shoulder, smell his Tide detergent and drive back to Woods Hole. I wanted to go to The Clam Shack with a bottle of French rose and eat fried clam strips and hot dogs on the rooftop, fending off the seagulls. I wanted to get a margarita at Shuckers and a bowl of creamy chowder from The Leeside. I wanted to lay in Jeff's living room and listen to music in the dark. I wanted to...I stopped. I couldn't go any further with this fantasy. Jeff was engaged and I was living with Stephen. We were just friends, that's all, the end.

"No, I'll be okay. I should go talk to him and straighten this out. I probably shouldn't even have told you since it's most likely nothing."

"I'm glad you did. Call me if you need me."

"Thanks. Say hello to Jessica for me."

"Whatever," he laughed. "Talk to you later."

When I hung up the phone, I felt really alone, in like *The Day After* way alone...the last man standing. I looked down at my remaining compadre, Dingo. He was still lapping up dirty frozen yogurt from the sidewalk. At least I had him.

When I got home from my walk, Stephen was sitting on the couch in the dark. His face was lit up by the bowl of pot he was smoking. The room reeked like a college frat house. He was always a big pot smoker, but I guess I'd forgotten that, or I didn't so much mind before. Now, it seemed to me that he was a bit too old to be sitting around smoking a big dubie in the middle of the day--borderline pathetic.

"What's up?" I said, fanning my hand back and forth across my face to breathe.

"Not a whole lot," he said.

"I gathered. You okay?" I couldn't believe *I* was actually asking *him* if he was okay.

"Yeah, why? Just chillin' out and thinking about things."

That sounded extremely loaded. I took the bait. Maybe a shower confessional was coming?

"Things? Like what?"

"I think I am going to quit Spolinni's. I need to focus more on my acting."

Of course I should have known that his thinking about things didn't include us. I was the only one who ruminated constantly about the state of our relationship. Some things didn't change.

"Well, you are focused on your acting. You've been going to some auditions at Actors' Equity, haven't you? And what about your class?" Stephen actually had not gone on many auditions, from what I could tell. All the auditions at Actors' Equity started at 10 o'clock in the morning, and the line outside the building waiting to sign up for these open calls started as early as 6 a.m., particularly if it was for Lincoln Center or the Roundabout Theatre. Stephen was deep in REM sleep at that hour.

"I just feel like I need to get rid of everything comfortable in my life to really give me the drive to succeed. Like, I'm thinking of getting rid of the apartment too…"

Okay, easy. Ghandi. What the F?

"Um, Stephen, I live in this apartment too. What are you talking about?"

"No, I know. I don't know what I'm saying. This set up is just all too comfortable, and it's in the discomfort that you find your creativity."

I hated when he waxed all philosophic, especially since the only literature he read was *Moby Dick,* and he got through about two chapters of it before putting it aside to read yet another play. I looked around the room for the Self-Help for Actors book.

"Well, don't let me keep you here, trapped in the comfort," I said.

"You're not. Relax, Emma. Not everything is about you. This is about me...my craft..."

UGH! I hated him! Why was he doing this again? And the g "c" word! Brutal.

"I'm not saying everything is about me, Stephen! I just can't help but look out for myself. I think I have good reason to."

"Are you ever going to get over the past? I said I was sorry."

"Well actions speak louder than words, and yours right now feel eerily similar to the past. It's scaring me." I started to cry. I wasn't going to hide it. Stephen's face shifted and he became noticeably softer.

"I'm sorry, Bunny. Come here," he said, getting off the couch, reaching for me with both arms outstretched. He looked like Frankenstein when he took his first steps. I melted into his arms. He smelled like pot and green Speed Stick deodorant.

"I just don't know what's going on here," I said.

"Me neither. But I know I love you."

I didn't say it back. I wanted to, I think...but I held back.

"Did you have sex with someone in the shower at The Gansevoort?" I blurted it right out, no mincing words.

"You read my index cards."

"Yeah, I read your cards! Well, did you?"

"I'm not going to indulge your paranoia, Emma," he said taking a hit off his joint. Holding the smoke in his lungs, he managed to eek out the words, "You should know the answer to that." Huge exhale and a cloud of smoke filled the room.

"Well, I guess I don't. So did you?"

"No, I did not. It was a reference to a play I read, okay?" He abruptly switched on the light. It looked like a cheap motel room, and I felt like we were a couple of junkies, except that I was completely sober. I didn't know whether or not to believe him, but I really had no choice. I had to take his word for it if I wanted to continue being with him. But did I want to? I felt so confused.

Chapter 13

There was a conference on eating disorders happening at NYU the following day, and Kimmie drove to New York to attend. I went to meet her in Washington Square during the lunch break. As I walked down University Street, I saw the white arches that mark the beginning of the park and thought about the movie *When Harry Met Sally.* In front of these arches was where they said goodbye after their cross country drive in the beginning of the movie. They had no idea at that point that they'd eventually become best friends and then get married. I thought about my friendship with Jeff and how it was too bad that we never got married. But things happen for a reason, and he was getting married in some pukey "green" wedding to Jessica in a mere few months, and I was still wasting my life with Stephen. Wait, did I really just admit that to myself, I wondered? Then I saw Kimmie running up to me with a soft pretzel in one hand and a Pink Lemonade Snapple in the other. She looked beautiful, as always, wearing a beige Armani silk suit with a cream-colored, ruffled Marc Jacobs blouse underneath.

"Hello, hello!" Kimmie said, wrapping both arms around my neck. I veered my head to the left, dodging potential yellow pretzel mustard in my freshly blown-out hair.

"You look snazzy," I said. "Bet you're the belle of the ball at the psych conference."

"Ugh, don't even talk to me about it. Such a snore...but, Dr. Manning is presenting later this afternoon, so that should be cool."

"Oh, I wish I had known!" I said.

"Really though?" Kimmie jibed. We broke out in laughter and started walking West, past the homeless men playing chess. Every time I passed these guys, I'd look for Bobbie Fisher.

"Want to grab a drink?" I asked.

"It's only noon."

"And?"

"Good point. Where to?" Kimmie said.

We walked down West 3rd Street, past the Blue Note where I had my first waitressing job in the city. How far I'd come since the days of my neon blue tuxedo, I thought. Well, not exactly how far, since really I hadn't gone anywhere--I was still here. But, rather, how fast time was flying by. I thought back to the first time I blew a bubble with chewing gum, a monumental incident in my life, my first memory. I was on our lavender, plush couch in the unlived in living room, and our Scottish terrier, Daisy, was with me. The bubble made a loud "crack!" and I jumped up, calling and calling for my mother. Daisy was running around in circles, reacting to my excitement. It was then that I realized my mother was not around. I was alone with no one but Daisy to share in my chewing gum victory. It was the first time I felt really alone.

Kimmie and I saddled up at the bar at DoWa, a Korean Barbecue spot that had remarkable martinis and mixed drinks. The naturally ordered a Grey Goose dirty martini and Kimmie got a passion fruit cosmopolitan. "Delish," she said, strategically placing the martini glass back on the grey, slate bar. "So how are things going with you? More importantly, how are things going with Stephen?" she asked.

"They're fine, I guess. I don't know. I don't know what I'm doing here anymore."

"Uh oh. Trouble in Paradise Lost?" she asked. Kimmie loved to make literary references. She liked to wear her ivy league education on her sleeve.

"So what's up with you? Met any saucy ladies in Provincetown?" I asked, deflecting her question.

"Well, I need to talk to you...about Jeff."

My heart momentarily stopped.

"Is he okay?"

"Well it depends how you define "okay." Physically, yes, but mentally is another story."

"What do you mean?" I asked.

"Well, he and Jessica called things off, as I'm sure you already know."

"What? No!" I was truthfully stunned. I felt the urge to walk to Port Authority and hop on the next Peter Pan bus to Woods Hole. "When?"

"Yeah… it was a few days ago…And, well…" she said, taking a sip of her passion fruit Cosmo, "it's because of you." She took a bite out of her orange slice garnish, staring at me, and waited for my reaction. I felt scared, guilty and elated all at the same time. I was desperate to hear more.

"What do you mean? What happened?" I asked.

"Well, it's kind of a long story…but, long story short, I made the mistake of talking to him one night and telling him how you missed him and how you wondered if you'd made a huge mistake by leaving."

I started mentally scanning the emails I'd sent Kimmie, what I had said about Jeff. Was nothing sacred?

"Well what does that have to do with Jessica and him?"

I was sort of playing dumb here but needed more info. I

looked to the bartender who was reading *Backstage* at end of the bar and signaled for another round.

"Well, he pressed me for what was going on with you and Stephen, and I don't know, I guess I told him that you were miserable."

"Kimmie! I am not *miserable*; I am *acclimating*. It's a drastic life change! How could you go telling him that?" I screamed.

The bartender looked at me with pity, frowning, and a waitress with hot pink streaks in the front of her black bob stopped doing her roll-ups. "But, wait, what'd he say?"

"Well, he'd had about five grapefruit gimlets...so he wasn't extremely coherent when he confessed all this to me, but he told me that he thought you had made a huge mistake and that he couldn't get you off his mind. He's in love with you, Emma."

Just hearing the words that Jeff was in love with me made me want to leap off my bar stool and skip down Carmine Street. In that instant, I had clarity. All the rumination and second-guessing were gone. I knew what I wanted, and I didn't have to ask anyone else's advice about what I should do, for once. I wanted to see Jeff. I wanted to be with Jeff. I wanted to go home, to Woods Hole. That was where I belonged.

"Did he say that? That he was in love with me?" I asked.

"Sort of...I kind of said it for him, based on what he was spewing."

"Wait, so...hold on. He never actually said this?" I spiked an olive in my martini with a toothpick.

"Not totally...But, Emma, he is in love with you! You belong together. This thing with Stephen is bullshit. You should come home and be with Jeff."

I was extremely irritated and now getting pissed off. "Kimmie, if he never actually *said* anything, I hardly think I'm going to move home to be with him. For Christ's sake, maybe things are going great with Stephen. How would you even know?"

"From your emails! It's so obvious he doesn't make you happy." She knew she had just shit stirred, because she started folding her cocktail napkins into miniscule squares and avoided making eye contact. She was clearly uncomfortable.

"Um, you don't have your Ph.D. in psychology yet, so I think you can save the psychoanalysis. Kimmie, don't bud in where you don't belong." I grabbed a handful of wasabi peas from the bar and bit one in half. Why were these popular, I wondered? They're so dry and spicy.

"Fine. I guess I thought you'd be happy, but I guess I thought wrong."

"Yeah, you did," I scowled back. I was hurt and embarrassed. "Please, save the drama for the psych unit. I certainly don't need it."

We finished our drinks mostly in silence and parted ways.

I started walking uptown to Stephen's apartment and felt flush, irritable and despondent. Why was everything so complicated?! Why couldn't everyone just leave me alone?

∧

A week went by in New York where I really tried to get a job and make a life for myself there again. I wanted to put the Jeff and Kimmie conversation behind me and try to focus on Stephen and making things work. After all, I hadn't really given it a fair shot, and Stephen seemed to be making an effort. I registered with Office Team and Man Power to get temp work and scheduled a timed typing test. They told me I also had to take an Excel and Microsoft Word familiarity exam at their downtown office. Though I felt pretty confident that I knew Excel, having done 10,000 spreadsheets at the

Chelsea perfumery back in the day, I barely passed the exam---deeming me Excel-inept.

"Well this really is going to limit your hourly pay," Vanessa, the Office Team HR rep told me. "Excel is a basic skill that employers expect you to have these days."

"But I know how to do a spreadsheet. I just don't know how to do all that other funky stuff--the shortcuts--that no one ever asks you to do."

I was getting surly. I mean, was $15 an hour really that much to ask for someone who graduated from Northwestern on the dean's list and had a decade of administrative assistant's work under her belt? I thought most temps were nothing more than glorified monkeys!

"Well your test results indicate that you're in the 30th percentile, meaning 70 percent of test takers scored higher than you." This was an all-time low, really.

"Well, are there jobs that don't require me to use Excel then?"

"Sure there are. Plenty. Let me take a look in my files." Vanessa started typing 90 miles per hour on her keyboard while I perused her office. She was planning a wedding, from what I could tell. Her pink and green "Wedding Day Planner" book was spread out behind her on the windowsill, as well as what looked like colored swatches for linen choices, also pink and green. I was guessing a July wedding in Nantucket.

"Getting married?" I asked. I attempted to ingratiate myself with Vanessa, hoping to grab that extra hourly buck.

"Yep." She kept typing, totally unengaged.

How was it, I wondered, that this less-than-friendly, kind of heinous woman was getting married and had the authority to dictate my pathetic hourly pay, when I was a struggling peon, jobless and single? What the hell happened here?!

"How are you with working with animals?" she asked.

"Great." At this point, anything would have been great. I did have that iguana when I was 20…and Dingo.

"Good. Well looks like I have an opening here for a three week assignment at the East Side Animal Hospital as a front desk receptionist."

"Sounds perf." I said.

"Excuse me?"

I always forgot that people didn't quite get my abbreviated language.

"Perfect."

∧

I was headed to meet Kara for a cocktail at The Mermaid Inn on East 5ᵗʰ and Second Avenue when Jeff called.

"So I presume you heard the news?" he said.

"Kimmie told me. I'm really sorry to hear it."

"No you're not. You hated her." I laughed. He knew me too well.

"Well, I'm glad I don't have to wear that split pea soup number, I will say that. Hey, is she going to reimburse me?" I looked down at my feet and there was a Chihuahua in a pink fur coat growling at my ankles. I almost accidentally stepped on it. It was like the spirit of Jessica haunting me on Second Ave.

"Okay, Frugal Fannie, maybe you can get past yourself for a moment in my time of despair."

"Shit, yeah, sorry."

"I'm kidding. I'm fine. Really."

"So what happened? Did she think your EP scores were too low?"

"EP?"

"Earning Potential."

"Oh, right. Well, that's true. I don't have high-EP as a painter. But, actually, I was the one who ended it…not that that's really important." This news made me extremely happy. Not just because I didn't want Jeff to have to experience the emotional pain of being dumped on his ass, but also because Jessica deserved it. She didn't appreciate him and was a gold-digging, vegan user. Just sayin'…

"So what made you do it?" I stopped and stood in front of Kabin. It was an old tavern made of dark brown wood resembling a log cabin. Shitty bar, but good beers on draft. Any bar that served Magic Hat #9 was top-notch.

"I don't know. It just wasn't right. Guess I knew that from the beginning, but I thought maybe I just had cold feet and that things would change once we were engaged."

I remembered how my mother had once proposed this to me. More like, she proposed to me for Stephen. She thought Stephen and I should just get engaged and that would make all of our problems go away. She even offered him up her old engagement ring from my father while at our Annual 4th of July picnic. Sometimes I blamed her that he dumped me only a few weeks later over his bowl of Honey Bunches of Oats.

"So how'd she take it?" I asked Jeff.

"I wouldn't say well, but she's okay. She's leaving the Cape."

This news made me even more happy. Jessica poisoned Woods Hole, like a noxious school of fish in Eel Pond. Okay, maybe that's a bit harsh, but all the same, I was pleased by the news of her exile.

"So you mean it's safe for me to come visit?"

"I'd love it if you did. Anytime."

I seriously considered jumping on the Peter Pan bus at Port Authority right at that moment. It would only be five hours till I could see Jeff again. I missed our daily chats and our five o'clock cocktail. I missed everything about him, so much that it almost hurt. Where was all this coming from, I wondered. It's like I kept it all pent up inside, and it was rushing out. A waitress came out of Kabin and stood next to me lighting up a smoke.

"Well, maybe... I kind of have some stuff going on here right now."

"By stuff you mean Stephen?"

"Well, that, and I got a job...at an animal hospital." I paced back and forth and stepped on a piece of sticky, hot chewing gum. "Shit."

"I hope you're not cleaning out cages. Wait, remember your Iguana?"

"Totally. He's how I got the job. Sort of…Anyway, no, not cleaning cages. Front desk work as a temp. I don't know what the fuck I'm doing with my life. How did this happen to me? I used to like ride the high school float and now I'm single, wrinkled, and working as a temp at an animal hospital in my 30s."

"Did you really ride your high school float?"

"No. We didn't have one. But if we did, I'd sure as hell have been riding it," I said, scraping the gum off the sole of my shoe with a pencil.

"Like Sandra Bullock?"

"In *Hope Floats*!" We laughed. Jeff and I watched *Hope Floats* together late one night on the Oxygen channel, another one of my faves. I convinced him that it was a good movie and made him sit in anguish and watch it in entirety. He got me back though by insisting that he had the right to choose the next three movies we rented at Blockbuster, "as penance" for what I made him endure. They were all action films…definitely not my fave.

I looked up and saw Kara standing in front of The Mermaid Inn. I wasn't ready to hang up.

"I'm sorry, Jeff. I have to run. Kara's meeting me, and she's standing in front of the restaurant flagging me down and pointing to her imaginary wristwatch."

"No worries. Call me soon."

"Okay. I'll call you tomorrow. Okay? Just to check in on you."

"I'm fine, really. Say hello to Kara for me."

"Okay, talk to you tomorrow," I said.

When we hung up, I felt like a part of me was truly missing. That part of me was Jeff….he was, as Shel Silverstein called it, my Missing Piece.

Kara and I saddled up to the bar at Mermaid Inn and ordered two glasses of the Oyster Bay Sauvignon Blanc. I started inhaling the bowl of Goldfish crackers set out on the bar.

"Hungry?" Kara asked. "Jeez, what are you, pregnant?"

"Knock on wood!" I scolded her. "God, I hope not!"

"Things going that well with Stephen?" She laughed. I did not.

"No."

"Wait, I was kidding. Seriously? Are you okay?"

"I don't know," I said and bit the orange head off the goldfish. The crumbs fell onto my lap and settled in the pleats of my Club Monaco silk black skirt. "I think I want to go home."

"Home? Wait, where, to your apartment? Do you feel sick?"

"No, home…I mean the Cape." The bartender flashed me a smile and refilled our bowl of crackers. I assured him we were going to order appetizers too--not just chow the freebies.

"Since when is the Cape home?"

"I just don't feel right here. Things don't feel right. It feels forced," I said, "And I don't belong here anymore. I belong in Woods Hole."

"Okay, hold on a minute here, Little Miss Cape Cod. Did you and Stephen get into a fight? I am sure you can work it out without having to move! I mean, you just got here!"

"Kara, stop thinking about yourself here. This is about me, and I'm telling you that I'm unhappy."

Kara knew I was right. She dropped her head in defeat. "I can't believe this is happening again. I feel like I was just getting used to having you back…now you're leaving me again."

"I don't know. I'm not leaving yet. I'm just saying I'm thinking about it." I swigged the remainder of my

Sauvignon Blanc. "I need something stronger, like a dirty martini."

I was on a mission to get drunk and numb the pain and confusion I was feeling. Jeff was no longer with Jessica, but he wasn't with me. And I was with Stephen, but he wasn't really with me either. He was, and always would be, I realized, with himself. Not only did I not love Stephen anymore, but I barely even liked him. In fact, everything about him at that moment irked me.

"He's a complete fraud," I spat, as my tongue got thicker and thicker.

I told Kara about the index cards, about the hot air he talked about going on auditions, about the affected way he carried Bukowski poems around with him, about his journaling and haikus.

"He is a loser, Emma. I hate to say it, but I've always thought so," Kara said. "This just confirms it."

I had done the unthinkable--told my girlfriend about all of the things I hated about my boyfriend, all the horrible dark secrets about our relationship. Now if we stayed together, he stood no chance of regaining favor in her eyes.

"Why didn't' you tell me?" I said.

"I tried to, but you wouldn't listen. You were so wrapped up in him. It's like you were blind."

I was blind, but now I could see...Isn't that a saying somewhere, I wondered? Polishing off another dirty martini, I decided to head home to talk to Stephen. Maybe not such a good idea two 'tinis and a glass of wine down, but, hey, when I wanted to do something, I needed to do it right away. Pull the Band-Aid off--tear it off, more like it--and do it quick.

Chapter 14

Stephen was not in the apartment when I got home. He decided to go for an after-work drink with some of the waiters from Spollini's. Impulsively, I called him on his cell. I wanted to get some things off my chest, confirm that things were not working out, and it seemed imperative that I couldn't wait till morning.

"I need to talk to you," I slurred.

"Well, can't it wait till I get home?" Stephen said. "I just ordered another beer."

"Fine," I said and hung up the phone. I was too tired to fight and honestly felt like puking. I wasn't sure if it was all the drinks or the idea that I'd made an egregious mistake by coming back here and moving in with Stephen.

When I woke up in the morning, Stephen was still not home. He had left me a voicemail that he and his friend Ziggy went to grab breakfast at The Coffee Shop in Union Square. He had stayed out drinking till morning and needed to sober up with a cheddar and bacon omelet. Still groggy, I got out of bed, as I was due to be at The East Side Animal Hospital in an hour and still had to make my way across town and up 30 blocks, not an easy commute. I showered quickly, more like did a glorified sponge bath, and put on my go-to "first day of work" outfit: my gray Old Navy slacks and my white French Connection ruffled blouse. This was what I had worn my first day at Cape Cod Hospital. I remembered Robin telling me that she had the same shirt in pink when I first met her.

When I got to the animal hospital, my supervisor greeted me at the front desk where I was to perch for three weeks.

"Hi, Emma," she said. "I'm Alice Taylor. I'll be supervising you this week." Alice was a vet tech, and she wore blue scrubs, like a surgeon, except her scrubs had little daisies on them. Her hair was graying at the temples, and I guessed she was about 42. No wedding ring. I wondered if she had like 20 cats in her apartment, and maybe a stray turtle or two. Alice went over my daily responsibilities, including registering patients and their pets, cleaning the waiting room, and maintaining the database, and she showed me how to use the phone. At 9 o'clock, the place was buzzing, as was my hungover head. Dogs, cats, birds…you name it. One woman even brought in a baby bat she found in her attic. The animals were sick and squawking in the waiting area. I looked over at a Dachshund, whose long face and floppy ears reminded me of Dingo. He had kidney disease and a respiratory infection and the doctors said his days were numbered. I couldn't hold it together. I started crying at the desk and wondered if I'd be able to make it a whole three weeks without breaking down every time a new patient came in.

The day flew by, as I was busy answering phones and escorting animals to the scale behind the front desk to be weighed for their charts. By far, the most interesting patient of the day was the short-eared mother owl that had fallen out of a tree. Who knew there were even owls in New York City…other than night owls at the bars, I guess. I sympathized with the little owl, feeling as if I had fallen out of my tree as well. That, and I too have small ears. By five o'clock, I was exhausted but anxious about going home to see Stephen. I knew we had a lot to talk about, but I just wasn't prepared to tell him that I was no longer in love with him. It seemed too cruel. After all, he was trying. He couldn't help it that he sucked; he just did.

I decided to walk home, giving me time to think and prolong the disaster that awaited. Walking cross-town on 59th Street, I wondered whether I was making a mistake. I mean, I was in love with Stephen for the past four years, wasn't I? All I wanted was for him to love me back, and now he did, and it was simply not enough. Was I being rash, needy, harsh? I passed the Russian Tea Room on my right, where Stephen and I spent a lavish evening ordering Oysters and various types of fruit-infused vodka. I remembered us being so drunk from drinking cranberry infused vodka one night that Stephen tripped and literally fell on top of me, pushing me to the floor. The only thing to break his fall was unfortunately my wrist and forearm, which had a silver cuff bracelet on it that had to be basically surgically removed and was bent beyond recognition. My mother had given me that bracelet at graduation. I still have it, and it's still bent.

My cell phone rang. It was Stephen.

"Hey, you coming home soon? I miss you," he said.

"Yeah, I'm on my way now." My stomach sunk.

"Where were you all day?" he asked. See, this was the problem. He was so self-involved that he didn't even remember I had gotten the temp job at the animal hospital. In fact, I wasn't sure he'd even known about it at all, as we rarely talked about me. This was par for the course for Stephen. He still called Kara, "Jane," because he never took the time to get to know her or listen to my stories about her.

"I was on the East Side. I'll be home soon," I said and hung up the phone.

As I neared the apartment, I became increasingly agitated and anxious. I passed the deli where the clerk had asked Stephen and me if we were married. I wondered if maybe I should inform him that, no, that was never going to happen. I reached back into my backpack to refresh my lip gloss and freshen up from the long, sweaty walk home. When I turned the corner onto 56th Street, I saw someone sitting on our front stoop. From afar, I couldn't make out his face. I was like Velma on *Scooby Doo* when I didn't wear my glasses--blind as a bat when it came to face recognition beyond five feet.

As I got closer, the man on the stoop stood up and looked increasingly familiar with every step of the way…Finally I made out his form and face…one very familiar…it was Jeff.

"Hey, stranger," he said.

"Oh my God! What are you doing here?" I ran to him for a hug. I held on tight, soaking in his familiar scent of Tide and Finesse shampoo.

"I came to get you," he said.

"What do you mean?" I said, pulling back from the hug.

"I'm taking you home. With me. To Woods Hole. Today."

I started laughing and crying at the same time. I wanted to say something, think of all the reasons why I couldn't go, but I didn't have any. It seemed so right.

"Is that okay with you?" he asked.

I was stunned to silence, elated and confused all at once.

"I think that's a good thing," I said.

"Yeah. This whole New York thing? Bad call," he said. "Just sayin'…"

We laughed. And then we kissed.

"Does Stephen know you're here?" I asked, looking up to the fire escape outside our apartment window.

"Yeah, I kind of just told him I'm taking you with me."

"Shut up! You did not…did you? Wait, what'd he say?" In that instance, I realized I didn't really care what Stephen had to say.

"Well, he accepted it. He really had no choice. You belong with me, Emma. You're mine."

I looked into Jeff's eyes. He was right. I was his. And he was mine.

"I started packing your things, but I ran out of trash bags."

"God, for a girl with baggage, I have ironically run out of bags."

"Let's get out of here," he said.

But I felt like I owed it to Stephen to say goodbye. After all that we'd been through, he deserved an explanation. When I got upstairs to the apartment, he was writing a new index card and had a carton of Hefty trash bags on his lap.

"Hey," I said.

Stephen looked up at me, and at that moment he looked very small, like a young boy. I felt sorry for him in this dark apartment. He seemed so alone. How the tables had turned.

"So I guess you talked to Jeff?" I said.

"Yeah, I guess I did," he said. "I went out and bought you more trash bags, if that's what you really want…if he's what you really want, I mean."

I didn't say anything and just looked down at the floor-- the dirty maroon carpet. I knew in my heart that Jeff was what I wanted, but I felt so guilty and terrible leaving Stephen like this.

"I don't know. I mean, it's not necessarily I want him over you, you know? I guess this just isn't working with us. I'm not working with us...you know? I think I've changed," I said.

"I knew this would happen someday," Stephen said.

"You knew what would happen?"

"I knew you'd realize how great you were, and I'd lose you," he said.

Stephen was right. For once in my life, I felt good about who I was and what I was doing. I may not have been the next Nobel Laureate or the next Tony Award-Winning actress, but I was me, and that was enough. I didn't need him--or even Jeff--to feel good about myself. I needed me on my side, and now I was.

"I'm sorry, Stephen," I said.

Stephen helped me pack up the rest of my things. Jeff waited with Dingo on the front stoop, watching the car while we went back and forth up the five flights. After bringing the last bag down, Stephen went to grab a pack of cigarettes and I went back upstairs to the apartment for one final look. This was it, I thought--the last time I'd be in Stephen's apartment. Would we ever be friends again, I wondered? Would he ever have a place in my life after today? As I was about the close the door behind me, I spotted the index card he had just written laying out on the sofa. I couldn't resist reading it: "The one that got away. Unmistakable regret."

I lay the index card back down and blew the flame out on the blue Glade candle. My cell phone rang.

"You okay?" Jeff asked. "Need me to come in a get you?"

"No, I'm okay," I said. "I'm more than okay. I'm great. Let's go home."

And with that, we went home...to Woods Hole...

Afterward

After moving back to Woods Hole, Jeff and I got engaged. He proposed on the rooftop cafe of The Clam Shack over a bottle of rose champagne and a fried clam strip plate. We got married the following summer in a small backyard wedding--no "green" theme. Kimmie and Kara were bridesmaids, and Dingo was the ring bearer. My mother and Ron made a wedding toast and announced their own engagement at the rehearsal dinner. My father and I danced to Frank Sinatra's "Summer Wind," his favorite song. Martin, Ricky Coldcuts, Dr. Manning, Claire and Robin all attended. I got my job back at the Eating Disorders Unit and am waiting to hear about acceptance to Ph.D. programs in Clinical Psychology. Jeff continues to work at the religious book publishers and paint. He has a gallery showing in Edgartown on Martha's Vineyard this October. Jessica is still gold-digging for someone with high EP. Stephen emailed me when he heard that I got engaged. He continues to work on his "craft" and pound the pavement pursuing a theatre career in NYC.

51297693R00165

Made in the USA
Middletown, DE
09 November 2017